STEPDADDY SEASON

NATISHA RAYNOR

Published By: K. Renee Publications

Chapter One

CYPHER

I heard a dish shatter in the distance as it hit the floor in the kitchen. The plate hitting the tiled floor was the perfect depiction of my mood because my heart shattered the moment my bitch of a boss told me that we were short-staffed, and I couldn't leave to go to my kids' football game. It was the second game of the season and the second one that I'd missed. And when I miss their games, there's way more that comes with that than just being sad and disappointed. It causes me to remember that their father isn't shit. It makes me recall how I hate him, and most days, I wished I had never met him. But then I wouldn't have my boys.

The almost constant guilt that comes with being a single mother is enough to stifle my breathing and make me dizzy with regret some days. I hated not being there for my boys because they already didn't have him. Knowing that when they were adults, their childhood memories would consist of both parents missing pivotal moments in their lives made tears fill my eyes. I didn't think I was being dramatic. I felt my feelings were valid, and as I snatched up the tray with my table's orders on it, the thought of walking out of the door crossed my mind. I wanted so badly to say fuck this job and go cheer my twins on as they dominated the field, but I had paid rent earlier, and doing so, left me with $175 in my checking account.

We needed food, and I needed gas. The light bill was also coming up due, and I didn't get paid from my full-time job for another two weeks. I could walk out the door and go be there for my sons, but the gratification would be short-lived once I was scraping pennies together trying to survive. The only thing I liked about being a waitress was that I left the job with money every day. The $193 worth of tips in my pocket was going to be used for grocery shopping the following day, so I needed to stay put. If I used coupons and was very selective with the items that I chose, I could use whatever I made at work tonight to buy groceries for the next three weeks at least, and that would be one less worry swimming around in my head.

Murmurs filled the room and the mixture of food, cologne, and perfume invaded my nostrils. The restaurant that I waitressed in part-time was always busy and that meant that tips were usually pretty good. If I went to work broke and left with a few hundred dollars in my pockets, that was always a win. My full-time job is at a call center and truth be told, I hate that job too. I hate customer service period because I get yelled at frequently for things that aren't even my fault. Most days, I can grin and talk shit in my head while ignoring it, but some days, I want to rip people a new asshole. I refrain, however.

My full-time job only covers rent and my car payment, so it's waitressing that keeps me afloat. I usually work a little overtime at the call center job when I have extra expenses approaching. Like the taxes on my car, school shopping for the boys, football expenses, etc. To sum things up, I feel like all I do is work and with raising eight-year-old twins, I be muhfuckin' tied. Yes, tied. But my boys are all I have, and I'm all I have. No one goes to bat for me like I go to bat for myself. I can get tired, and I can get frustrated, but I simply can't afford to quit. If I do, those children that didn't ask to be here suffer in the end.

My parents have suggested more than once that I come live with them for a year and save the money to buy a home. As tempting as that sounded, nothing would make me feel more pathetic than moving back home at thirty-two years old. I knew if I put my pride to the side it would help me in the long run, but I just wasn't feeling that. Plus, I wasn't even sure I wanted to be a homeowner because as with everything in life, expenses came with that too. Being a single mother was some bullshit in every aspect. I used to pray for a man to come save me, but after a few years of that, it dawned on me that no one was coming, and I had to save my damn self.

I took my table their food, dropped the tray back off to the kitchen, and went to the bathroom. Thankfully, it was empty, and I had a few moments to myself. I stared at my reflection in the mirror and wondered if this would always be life. Would I always work just enough to get by and maybe have some extra money left over for things that I liked like getting my nails done and buying new shoes? Would there always be something for me to sacrifice? Would I ever be truly and genuinely happy?

I pushed out a deep sigh as I used my fingers to sweep up the stray hair that had come out of the low bun that my hair was slicked back in. Getting my hair done is often a luxury that I can't afford, so a slicked back, low bun, with a swooped bang is damn near my signature style. Sometimes, if I'm feeling really fancy, I'll blow it out and wear it straight for a day or two. My hair hangs just past my shoulders. I learned to do my own lashes, so I don't always look so plain, and I didn't care how broke I was, I got my nails and feet done monthly. That was the one thing I refused to give up because damn, didn't I deserve to treat myself sometimes?

I'm 5'4 with reddish-brown hair and caramel-colored skin. I can't even afford the $195 right now for a yearly supply of contacts lenses, so I wear my black framed eyeglasses every day now. I had already missed two of my kids' games, so I was reluctant to sign up for overtime at the call center, but I needed some money. I only had $100 in my savings account. Financially, I felt like I was drowning.

My co-worker, Lucinda came in the bathroom and did a double take when she saw me. "Hey, boo. I thought you were going to the kids' game?"

I simply shook my head. If I had to say the words out loud, I just might cry. I pulled my phone from the pocket of my apron and shot my best friend, Kimbella a quick text asking her to please go be there for the boys for me. My mom was dropping them off at the game, but she couldn't stay either because my father had physical therapy, and she had to take him.

Lucinda kissed her teeth. "Let me guess, that bitch ass Linda said you couldn't go? I hate her ass. When is the next game?"

I typically work 3-4 nights a week at the restaurant because the money I make there pays my utilities and covers other small expenses. If I can make at least $400 a week, I'm good. The amount of money that I leave with each night is never guaranteed, but I can usually make at least $100 a day.

"Saturday," I replied as Kimbella texted me back and told me that she'd go be there for the boys. That made me feel a little better, but I was still down.

"You on the schedule?"

"The game is at noon, and I don't come in until three." I could barely even get a full weekend with my boys. I was always at one of my damn jobs, and I was sick of it.

"Bet. Next time they have a game, if I can take your shift, I will. Just let me know."

That got a smile out of me, and I glanced over at her. "I appreciate that, Lucinda. Thank you so much. Let me get back because I'm sure folks are looking for me." I rolled my eyes.

It was crazy to me how people I'd known a year or less had done more to make my life easier or help me with my boys than their own father. I had my kids when I was twenty-four, so I wasn't exactly a child, but I obviously still had some learning to do. I met Nick when I was nineteen, and we just had a sexual relationship for a year. He was always in between jobs, full of lies, bullshit, and excuses, and really not good for anything but dick. I was young and carefree and didn't really care because as soon as I got rid of one nigga, I added another one to my team.

When I should have been attending somebody's

college or thinking about a good, stable career, I was just out in the streets living my best life, and Nick didn't like that shit. It finally seemed that he got it together and got a good paying job at a warehouse. He started taking me out on dates and buying me things and when I got a decent paying job at Fed Ex sorting packages, we moved in together. Two months later, I was pregnant and three months after that, he was back jobless and back on his best bullshit.

Living with Nick for that year while I waited on the lease to be up was hell. The twins got everything they needed because of me, my parents, and the gifts I got from the baby shower. The entire time I was pregnant, the only thing Nick purchased was two boxes of diapers. The month after I had the twins, the lease was up, and I was broke, and had to move back home with my parents. I stayed at home with the boys for three months while I waited for my name to be reached on the daycare assistance list.

Once they were able to go to daycare, I went back to work, and I saved my money for six months before I felt I was ready to move out on my own. I was financially secure for all of three months before I was broke and living paycheck to paycheck again. Nick barely called the boys, rarely visited, and gave me money never. I hadn't seen him in almost five months, and I honestly didn't care. On their last birthday, Nick's mom dropped off two birthday cards with $25 inside each one. She's about as lame as her son, but she does pop out a few times a year and does something.

I've dated since I had the boys, but I kept hitting dead ends. I always ran into the men that wanted to sit up at my apartment and chill rather than taking me out on dates, and I've made it clear many times that wasn't an option. I wasn't bringing random ass men up in my home around my kids. Especially when they couldn't even come like gentlemen and wine me and dine me. Every time I started talking to a guy, I'd find out two or three months later that he had a girlfriend, or was a liar, was broke, or needed somewhere to live, and I was honestly over it. And with the way I work, I try to give all my free time to the boys, so I don't have time for a man anyway. I barely even have time for myself.

"Have a good night, Cypher," my bitch of a manager gave me a tight smile as I clocked out two hours later, and I ignored her. Fuck her.

I made my way out to my car and glanced over at the Lowe's Food across the parking lot. When I felt guilty, I bought my boys things and tonight, I wanted to take them cake and ice cream. I felt that was the least I could do. Lowe's Food is a little on the expensive side, so I don't go my grocery shopping there, but I grabbed a small cake, some ice cream, and a few snacks for the boys.

My mom had picked them up from their game, and she only lived five minutes from my job, so I was there in no time.

"I thought you were coming to the game, ma." Qori was on me as soon as I walked in the door.

"I thought I was too. I'm sorry. Someone didn't come to work, and my boss made me stay, but I promise I'll be there, Saturday." I hated breaking promises to my boys because the last thing I ever wanted to come off as was a liar. Their father did enough of that.

Qori nodded, and I breathed a sigh of relief. I couldn't take it when they whined and made me feel worse. "Go get your shoes. I have ice cream in the car. Where's Quentin?"

"Right here." The spitting image of Qori appeared. "We won our game. Everybody was cheering for us."

I tried to woman up and keep the tears at bay, but the tightness in my chest was uncomfortable. "Congratulations, baby. And I'm going to be there cheering for you, Saturday. I promise."

By the time I moved out of the apartment that I shared with Nick during my pregnancy, I was so disgusted by him that I didn't feel sad at all during the breakup. I was actually elated to be done with his bum ass. So, I had never really experienced heartbreak. Not until I brought those boys into the world, and it dawned on me just how hard raising them with minimal help would be. My worst fear was messing up and scarring them for life. I didn't want to be the reason they grew up and treated women like shit. I didn't want them to have mommy issues, and I beat myself up every time I felt like I wasn't doing a good job. God help me.

Chapter Two

HOUSTON

I tried to relax my facial muscles as I approached the door of my nieces' school, but I was pretty sure I was frowning. I knew I was frowning because I was pissed. My oldest niece, Ominique had just come back to school off a three-day suspension, and she was about to be suspended again for fighting. How in the hell a nine year old got suspended at least once a month was beyond me. I had even put shorty in therapy, but it didn't seem to be working. She wasn't a bully to my knowledge or a disrespectful kid, but shorty had no patience and zero tolerance for bullshit. She wasn't the type that was gon' argue with you. As soon as you made her mad, she was rocking your shit, and while a part of me didn't want to punish her for that, I also didn't want to raise a sociopath. I loved that she stood her ground and didn't take any shit, but I was also smart enough to know that she had some underlying issues that I needed to address ASAP.

It's not even like I didn't know where the issues came from. I've been raising my two nieces for the past year because my younger sister committed suicide. Life became too hard for her, and she took herself out. What child wouldn't be affected by that? Omi became angry and her eight-year-old sister, Terrionna became quiet and withdrawn. I'm twenty-eight with no kids, so suddenly being thrown into the role of a full-time parent was overwhelming as hell, but I wouldn't have it any other way. I was already heartbroken that my sister didn't reach out to me for help before she made such a drastic decision. I would never let her kids down. That shit wasn't an option. So every time it got hard, I just had to roll my sleeves up, take a deep breath, man up, and handle that shit.

I walked into the office, and the receptionist who knew me, Omi, and Terrionna by name and face, smiled at me. She appeared to be in her mid-twenties and despite the wedding band on her finger, she flirted with me every time I came into the office.

"Hi, Mr. Robinson. The heavy weight champ is in with Ms. Lanier. You can go ahead back. I love those shoes." Her eyes trailed the length of my body. Her gaze stopped momentarily on my dick print and eventually, slid down to my shoes.

"Thank you." I tipped my head in her direction and headed for the office to deal with Ms. Omi.

"Anytime."

I could feel her eyes on me as I walked around the desk towards the office. Dealing with women in relationships has never been my thing because I'd hate to have to put a goofy ass nigga in the dirt behind a piece of pussy. I'm also in a relationship, and I don't cheat. I did when I was younger. I'd stick dick to anything with a fat ass and a pretty face. Really, the ass didn't even have to be fat. I was just a pussy hound, and during my senior year in high school, I had two girlfriends the entire year. I stand 6'5, and with my height, dark skin, and long wicks, I've never had a problem getting women.

When I met Tiesha two years ago though, I challenged myself to be faithful to her, and a nigga had done it. No matter how many women practically put my pussy in their hands, I always turned it down. I used my knuckles to tap on the principal's door and waited to hear the words *come in* before I entered. As soon as I opened the door, my gaze landed on Omi's face. It took everything in me not to smile because that little girl was the spitting image of my sister. Omi was her fucking twin. Looking at her made me smile, but that shit made my heart hurt at the same time. Every damn day I wondered why my sister left us. I didn't judge her or think negative thoughts about her because I knew my sister, and if she was hurting badly enough to leave her kids and her family, then she was hurting indeed.

Ms. Lanier was an older black woman, and I knew that she was trying to work with Omi without breaking the rules or showing favoritism. Anyone with a heart that knew what the girls had gone through tried to work with them, but at some point, enough had to be enough. She smiled at me, and I tipped my head in her direction.

"I'm sorry we have to keep meeting under these circumstances. What happened this time?" I looked over at Omi, who was still pouting with her arms crossed over her chest.

"Simone said she wanted to play mamas, and I told her I didn't want to play that game because it was childish. So, she said I didn't want to play because I didn't have a mother, and I asked her not to say that again. And she said it again," Omi stated unapologetically with her head held high. I could read between the lines, and she let it be known that ole girl got what she got, and Omi wasn't sorry for giving it to her.

Ms. Lanier peered over the rim of her glasses at Omi. "Ominique, we've discussed this many times. In life, people will always say things that we don't like. You can't hit a person every time they make you upset. You'll be fighting for the rest of your life. You have to learn how to ignore people. You just got back from being suspended, and I have to send you home for two more days, and I'm really supposed to be sending you home for ten. I can't keep bending the rules for you. You were supposed to be out of here two suspensions ago. One more suspension, and you have to leave here and go to alternative school for the rest of the year."

I glanced over at Omi and took in the stoic expression on her French vanilla-colored face. Omi had light skin, and Terrionna's skin was rich in melanin like me and my sister's. Omi and Terrionna's dad isn't exactly dark-skinned, but he's two shades darker than Omi. When she was a few weeks old, and he saw that she wasn't getting darker, he demanded a paternity test from my sister, but she was indeed his. Both girls have thick, curly hair, and are going to be tall as shit. They're both the tallest ones in their class.

It was obvious to me that Omi didn't care about going to alternative school, but I didn't want that for her. I didn't want her to be labeled as a bad kid and written off. But what could I do? I felt sorry because she'd lost her mother. I just didn't have it in me to punish her, but something was going to have to give. It had been a year, and sadly, Omi was going to have to find out that life goes on.

"Thank you for all that you've done," I directed

my attention towards Ms. Lanier. "If that's all, I'll take Omi now."

Ms. Lanier picked up a thick manila envelope and extended it towards me. "This is her work for the next few days."

"Thank you."

We walked out of the office and through the school doors. The walk to my red BMW was silent, and once we were inside the car with our doors closed, Omi spoke. "I asked her nicely not to say I didn't have a mother anymore."

My eyes shot up to the rearview mirror, and I peered at her reflection. "Omi, when kids get mad at each other, the first thing they do is crack mama jokes. You're only nine. You have a long way to go, and unfortunately, someone else is going to bring up your mother again. You're going to have to develop thick skin and stop letting every little thing set you off. You want to go to the school with the bad kids?"

Omi shrugged her shoulders aggressively while she stared out of the window and scowled. Shorty wasn't angry at the situation. She was angry at life, and she had every right to be, but she had to get it together. I hated to do it, but I was going to have to put my foot down and toughen up as well.

"No TV while you're suspended," I stated in a low tone. "No iPad, no cell phone, and you can't go outside and play. Got it?"

She turned away from the window and looked at me with hurt in her eyes. I wanted to look away because that puppy dog look was breaking me down, but I knew I had to stay strong. She was looking at me like I told her I was going to whoop her when we got home, but I understood. She wasn't used to being punished. I had been letting Omi's ass get away with murder.

"I'm on punishment?" she asked in a state of disbelief.

"Yeah, you are. I can't keep rewarding bad behavior. And instead of going to therapy once a month, I'm moving it up to every other week."

Omi stared at me for a moment, then she went back to looking out of the window. I was winging this parenting thing. I had no clue what I was doing, and my biggest fear was that I was going to let my sister down and screw her kids up.

* * *

"You going home?" I looked over at Tiesha as she got out of my bed and began picking her clothes up off the floor.

"Yes. When your alarm goes off, and you get up and start moving around getting the girls ready for school, it always wakes me up, and I can't go back to sleep."

I watched her get dressed while that familiar feeling crept into my stomach. I don't know what the shit is, and it's hard for me to describe, but every time Tiesha says something that makes it seem to me like she thinks my nieces are a burden, it makes me feel some kind of way. They aren't my kids, but I'll go to war about them and behind them, and anyone that isn't for them damn sure isn't for me. But I hated when Tiesha or any other females were sensitive as hell or overreacted, because I always make the effort to think rationally. I try not to assume and jump to conclusions, so I always attempted to make myself believe that it wasn't like that, and I was overreacting.

Tiesha works second shift at a call center, and she normally sleeps until about noon. She's a light sleeper and once her sleep is disturbed, it's hard for her to get back to sleep, so I never took it personal when she didn't want to stay over. But this time, my stomach felt like it was in knots. Like some shit wasn't right, but I wasn't sure if I should address it or leave well enough alone because I know how I am. I like being calm and laid back because once I'm mad, I can take it there. You think Omi is a live wire, I can get disrespectful as fuck, so I try to avoid confrontations. Tiesha and I had been together for two years, and even though I'd had my nieces for a year, I tried to tell myself that she was still adjusting.

She did come over that evening and cook dinner for us. I helped the girls with their homework, and Omi went to bed early since all her privileges had been revoked. I sat on the back porch and smoked a blunt while Tiesha cleaned up the kitchen, then I took a shower, and we had some good ass sex. It would have been cool to be able to wake up at three or four in the morning and slide back up in her for round two, but if she wanted to go home, I wasn't going to stop her.

Tiesha looked over her shoulder and caught me staring. She hit me with a small smile that showcased the dimple in her left cheek. "You like what you see?" she flirted.

"I do," I admitted. Tiesha used to run track in school, and even though she graduated six years ago, she still works out, and her body is athletic and toned. Her ass is a nice size, thanks to all the time she spends on the Stairmaster and all of the squats that she does. Tiesha looks good in anything that she wears, and my dick is always brick around her. With cinnamon-colored skin, and dark curly hair, she reminds me of Chili from TLC.

She put her shirt on and wiggled into her jeans before coming over to the bed and peering down at me. "You haven't taken me out in a minute. Can we do date night this weekend? I want to go to dinner."

"We can do that," I replied in a lazy tone, and that got a wide grin out of her. Tiesha leaned down and placed a juicy kiss on my lips. "I love you. Bye."

I sat up. "I love you too, and fuck is you saying bye for like I'm not gon' walk you to the door and out to your car?"

Tiesha didn't respond. She grabbed her things, and I followed her out the door, smacking her behind on the way. I walked her out to her Camry, and when she got in the car, I leaned in and kissed her once more. "Drive safe, and let me know when you make it home."

"I will, babe."

I closed her door and waited for her to pull off before I walked back inside the house. Before I got my nieces, Tiesha always hinted at us living together, but she hadn't mentioned it once since I had them. I did a damn good job of taking care of the girls, so I didn't *need* her to help me, but it would have been nice to have my girl there with us. She came through and cooked for us often, and she did the girls' hair whenever it wasn't braided or in some kind of protective style, but I didn't think she wanted to live in the house with us, and that was something else that made my stomach tight.

I didn't want to be that person to ignore signs and

red flags. Tiesha had never verbally expressed it, but I didn't think she was feeling the fact that I had taken my nieces in. I'm also smart enough to know that I hadn't confronted her about it because I knew if she confirmed my suspicions, she was going to have to get the fuck on because I'd never choose her over my nieces.

Chapter Three

CYPHER

Three days after I missed the boys' football game, I was walking into a popular tattoo shop in Diamond Cove, North Carolina, to get a tattoo for my birthday, which was Sunday. I was celebrating tonight, however, because Sunday was a school night, and it was very rare that I went out when my boys had school the next day. My parents had the boys, and I was trying to enjoy myself without feeling guilty about it. I had been saving for my birthday for two months. I got an outfit, some shoes, my hair done, and I wanted a tattoo. Kimbella was taking me to dinner, and we were going to the club afterwards.

I had paid a deposit for a large tattoo online, and when I thought about the fact that I was about to spend $100 on a tattoo, it was real hard not to chastise myself. I could be doing so many other things with $100, but on the other hand, I worked two jobs. I didn't deserve to treat myself for my birthday?

Kimbella and I walked into the tattoo shop that was located two miles away from the beach, and the soft sounds of rap music wafted from the speakers that were mounted on the wall and greeted us at the door. The shop was huge, very clean, and very nicely decorated. The floors were so shiny I could almost see my reflection in them. There were four tattoo artists that worked there, but I had booked my appointment with the owner, Houston. In order to make sure that I was able to get an appointment with him, I had to book three months in advance. He's like that. Damn near everybody in the city wants to be inked by him.

I looked at the pictures on the wall as the receptionist greeted me and Kimbella with a smile. Houston had done tattoos for several rappers, a few actors, and tons of athletes. I follow him on Instagram, and I knew there were times he'd close down the shop to the public, so celebrities could come through. Sometimes, he even traveled to where they were. He had a video on his page tattooing Lil' Durk in the studio. Houston is very talented, and I know celebrities don't hesitate to pay him to come to them or cater to them.

"Hiii, welcome to Inked by Houston. You have an appointment?"

I diverted my gaze to the pretty, brown-skinned receptionist. The super long, bone-straight Ginger wig she had on was fire, and she looked like she could be related to Teyana Taylor. She was stunning and friendly, so I smiled back at her.

"Yes. I have an appointment with Houston. I love your hair. That color is gorgeous on you."

"Thank you, boo." She beamed.

I saw a figure out of my peripheral vision, and when I looked that way, my knees buckled. Houston rarely posts pictures of himself on social media, but he had enough posted to where I knew he was fine, but damn! He was a ten in pictures but a twenty in person. He was talented indeed, but I now saw up close and personal why so many women made it their business to get tatted by him.

He had on gray sweatpants, and I'm ashamed at the way my eyes shifted downward until they landed on his dick print. Houston was heavier than a muhfucka between the legs.

"Here he is," the receptionist's voice snapped me out of the trance that I was in. "This is your next appointment, Houston."

My orbs lifted and landed on his face. "What's up? You can follow me this way."

"Got damn," I heard Kimbella mumble underneath her breath, and the only man her married ass openly marvels over is Damson Idris.

Houston led us down a short hallway into a medium sized room with more pictures of him and celebrities on the wall. This man had tatted almost every rapper in the game. The faint scent of weed lingered in the air, but the plug-in located in the socket by the door gave the room a vanilla smell. Houston's Creed cologne also tickled my senses. I could even smell the cinnamon from the Big Red gum he was chewing. All of the aromas together were like one big aphrodisiac.

His wicks gave me toxic vibes, and I knew he was probably the kind of man that would stress you out and make you lose a few pounds if your ass wasn't careful. I saw a Facebook meme once that said, the longer the wicks, the longer the lies. I believed it too. Houston was way too fine to be anything other than toxic, and about nine years ago, I probably would have been ready to play with fire fucking around with his sexy ass, but now, my single mother of two in my early thirties ass knew better. Way better.

"You have a picture of the tattoo that you want?" He asked as I sat in the tattoo chair.

"Yeah, I do." I unlocked my phone and went to my photo gallery.

"Where you getting it?" he asked as I showed him the photo of three butterflies that was saved in my phone.

"Right below my collarbone."

"I got you."

The way he said I got you, made my yoni contract. The timbre in his soft tone damn near drove me up the wall. It had been six months since I had sex, and the sex that I had back then wasn't anything to write home about. I was so over dating and meeting new men that every now and then, I let one of my old boo thangs spin the block just so I wouldn't have to add a new body to my list. I refused to deal with anyone married or in a relationship, so the pickings were slim. I hadn't been this aroused in a long time, and the man hadn't even done anything except speak to me.

"Can I see your phone?"

I passed it to him, and when my fingers brushed up against his, I swear I felt jolts of electricity. I had it bad, and I didn't even know this man. I've never in my life had a one night stand but a night with him was sounding like a birthday present that I would love to have.

Houston picked up a marker from the table that was beside him. "I don't have to use a stencil for this. I can freestyle draw it. You ladies from Diamond Cove?" he made conversation while he drew the butterflies on my body.

"Born and raised," Kimbella answered.

I tried to contain my nervousness. My heart was beating faster than normal, and I was afraid he'd be able to tell. The main reason I was nervous was because I knew the tattoos was going to hurt like crazy. I have the boys' names on my left arm, and they didn't hurt too bad, but I also knew that was because I had fat on my arm. The area below my collarbone didn't have an ounce of fat, and that shit was going to be excruciating. I knew it.

The second reason I was nervous was because this fine ass man was all up on me. Did I need some gum? Did I have something in my nose? I took pride in the fact that I'd never dealt with an ugly man, but this man was a different breed. He was one of those guys you saw on IG and Tik Tok with thirsty women going crazy in the comments. The kind that would have you having to check a bitch every other day. No thanks. I would for sure look, but I wasn't going to be crazy enough to bite the apple. I'm sure he wasn't checking for me anyway. I probably didn't even fit the aesthetic of the kind of woman that he went for.

"We should have taken a shot, friend. That's going to hurt," Kimbella noted as she peered over at the drawing on my skin.

"Please don't remind me," I groaned.

Houston's gaze lifted, and his eyes bore into mine intensely. "You scared?"

I swallowed hard, but it damn sure wasn't out of fear. I just wanted to suck on this man's bottom lip. If going long periods without sex was going to have me out here lusting like this, I needed to make it my business to get some D at least once a month. This was absolutely absurd.

"No, I'm not scared," I replied in a weak voice.

"This your first tat?"

"No. I have this one." I pointed to my arm, and his eyes scanned over the words. The tattoo artist I went to for that one damn sure wasn't as talented as Houston, but it didn't look like a jailhouse tattoo either. It was okay.

"Quentin and Qori. Those your kids?"

I smiled. "Yes. I have eight-year-old twins."

"Eight?" his eyes scanned my face. "You had 'em mad young? You barely look twenty-five."

I chuckled. "Thank you, but I wish. I turned thirty-three today."

"Damn." Houston's orbs trailed the length of my body in a lustful way that made my nipples harden. The way he was ogling me and the tone of his voice made me aware that he liked what he saw, and I damn sure took that as a compliment.

I sat there blushing like an idiot, and when he used the wheels on his chair to push himself backwards, Kimbella nudged me. She had peeped it too. Houston didn't stop rolling until he was close enough to the mini fridge in the room to open the door. He pulled out a bottle of 1942 and grabbed some clear plastic cups from the top of the fridge.

"If it's your G day, we definitely have to take some shots." He grinned, and I smiled back.

I wanted to scream out, '*Give me some birthday dick*!' but, I refrained.

Houston poured three shots and passed them out. "Cheers to another year." We clinked our cups and tossed back the shots. "What you doing for your birthday?"

"My friend here is taking me to dinner, and then we're probably going to the club for a few. That's about it. My sons have a football game tomorrow, and I have to work tomorrow evening, so I can't go too crazy."

"You have kids?" Kimbella asked, and I knew with that shot in her that her ass was about to start trying to play matchmaker. I cut my eyes at her. If Kimbella started her shit, I was going to be embarrassed. I'm sure thirsty women threw themselves at Houston every day. I didn't need my friend trying to pawn me off and letting him know just how pathetic my dating life was. I'm sure he had tons of options, and I pretty much had zero.

"I don't have biological kids, but I'm raising my nieces," Houston answered as he started picking up small vials of ink and placing them on his table.

"How old are they?" Kimbella kept it going.

"The oldest is nine, and the youngest one is eight."

"Interesting," Kimbella stated, and I turned to look at her.

"*Stop*," I mouthed, and she smirked.

A presence came to the door causing all of us to look in that direction, and a man as equally tall and fine as Houston was standing there. It was raining sexy, dark-skinned niggas with wicks around Houston's shop, and I wasn't mad at it.

"What's up?" The man spoke as he entered the room. "How long you gon' be in here tonight, bro?"

"My last appointment is at ten, and it's for a large tattoo, so I probably won't leave earlier than midnight. What's up?"

The guy leaned against the wall and started a conversation with Houston about his plans for the night. Then the topic was switched to everything from sports to cars. I loved listening to Houston talk, but there were some points in the conversation that I zoned out on because the tattoo I was getting hurt like a bitch. That one shot had done nothing to lessen the pain.

"You good?" Houston asked in a low tone as his eyes lifted, and he took in the scowl on my face. "You need another shot?"

"Yes please," I winced, and he chuckled. "Zeke, pour us up a shot of that 1942," he instructed his friend.

Zeke did as Houston requested, and I reached for

the cup he extended towards me fast as hell. I tossed the shot back with no hesitation and closed my eyes as Houston's needle hit a spot that made me want to jump out of the chair.

"You taking this shit like a champ," he complimented while my eyes were still closed.

"Am I? I'm sure I'm making some real ugly faces, but this shit hurts." My eyes were still closed, and I had a frown on my face. I'm not sure why I thought this was a good idea, but I wanted it to be over.

"I'm almost done with the outline. I just have to add the color after that."

Houston's voice was so soothing. I never wanted him to stop talking, but I couldn't tell him that. I liked hearing him talk to Zeke, but there was something about when he was speaking to *me*. It made me feel all warm and fuzzy inside. I racked my brain for something to say. I wanted him to keep the conversation with me going. Before I could think of anything my phone rang, and I opened my eyes.

Qori was calling me via facetime. I answered the call, and his pecan-brown face came into view. "Mommy," he gasped. "What are you doing? Are you getting a tattoo?"

"Yes. I am," I chuckled. "What are you doing? And anything other than getting ready for bed is the wrong answer."

"I wanted to ask you if you were coming to get us tonight," he whispered, making me laugh.

Qori and Quentin love my parents, but they love me more. When the boys act clingy, it warms my heart because it reminds me that, even though I have to work a lot, they still know it's us three until the world blows. I don't care who it is. My boys would choose me every time. They will go to my parents' house, run around in the yard, eat junk, and be spoiled, and still be ready to come home with me versus spending the night.

"No, because when Kimbella and I leave the club, it's going to be late, and you need to get your rest. You have a game tomorrow. I'm going to come pick you and your brother up in the morning, and we're going to go eat breakfast before your game. Okay?"

"Okay. Have fun at the club."

I smiled as I took in his frizzy braids. I had Sunday off from both jobs, and I was going to wash the twins curly, shoulder-length hair, and braid it. "Thank you. Where is your brother?"

"He's taking a shower. I'm next after him. Grandma ordered a pizza, and we had ice cream after we ate."

"Okay, I'm serious about you getting your rest. I want to see you play your very best tomorrow."

"Gotcha. I love you. Goodnight."

"Goodnight, baby." I smiled and ended the call.

No matter how hard being a single parent got, I never once regretted having my babies. Being pregnant with multiples and raising them is far from easy, but I'd do it ten times over again. I'd just choose a different man to have them with. My motherhood experience would be so much better if I had a partner to share the load with, but that was wishful thinking."

"All done." Houston snapped me from my thoughts, and I breathed a sigh of relief as he picked up a spray bottle, sprayed some liquid onto a paper towel, and wiped the tattoo off. Once the excess ink was removed from my skin, I looked down, and the tattoo was beautiful.

"I love it," I beamed. "Thank you."

Houston removed his gloves and tossed them in the trash. "Anytime."

I unlocked my phone and sent the rest of the payment via Cash App. His phone chimed, and he picked it up and looked at it. "Thank you. One more shot for the birthday chick?"

"Sure." I laughed as I picked up my empty cup.

Houston poured shots for me, him, and Kimbella, and we did another cheers before downing the shots.

"Thank you once again," I said as the shot of tequila went straight to my vagina.

Drinking and not having a dick to ride should be illegal. Especially when one of God's finest creations was the one pouring up the alcohol. I left Houston's shop, and as soon as we got in the car, Kimbella started.

"That man is fine as the fuck. He got me wanting a tattoo and shit."

"I know, right." I stared at the shop longingly. "I bet he has a girlfriend."

"I was about to ask. You know I wanted to, but I didn't want to hear your mouth. You need some new prospects on the team, Cypher. I get you not wanting to feel like a hoe and shit, but you can't keep doubling back to the same lame ass niggas you cut off. You see how it worked out when you let Nick double back. Niggas always want to come back when they see you doing good when they should just appreciate it the first time."

"You're right, and I get it but, that man in there, hell no. He looks like problems."

"He also looks like he'll stick his dick in your vagina, and you will feel it in your tonsils."

I erupted into laughter. "You are sick as shit."

Kimbella shrugged passively. "I'm just saying. Sometimes, you gotta be around for a good time and not a long time. Let a new man come in, tell you some good ole lies that will have you blushing, let him break that spine a few times, then send him back to the streets."

"It's just that simple, huh?" I chuckled.

"Damn right it is. It's only complicated when you

make it that way. Stop falling in love with these niggas, and just have a good time with their asses."

I rolled my eyes and glanced at her. "Says the woman with the ring on her finger."

Kimbella shrugged again. "And what was I out here doing before I met him, friend? Running the streets and giving these niggas hell."

I sighed. "Well, I don't have time to run the streets. I haven't been able to run the streets like that since I had kids, but I might not object to adding a lil' prospect to the team. I don't know who or when because these men out here are sick. All they wanna do is sit up on a chick's couch and watch her Netflix. I'd rather spend my nights alone than sexing a man that can't even take me to a nice dinner, a picnic, a midnight stroll on the beach, or something."

"I definitely don't want you to lower your standards. You don't have to rush it, but don't be closed off either. The right one will come along."

I wasn't so sure, but I was going to keep that to myself.

Chapter Four

HOUSTON

The sounds of Summer Walker filled my car as I gripped Tiesha's thigh with my right hand while the left hand rested on my steering wheel. I like all kinds of music. Rap music isn't the only music that I listen to, and at the moment, Summer was the vibe. Omi and Terrionna were with my mom, and after our date, I wanted to take Tiesha back to the crib and make her climb the walls as I gave her countless orgasms. I love my nieces. I wouldn't trade them for anything in the world, but sometimes, it felt good to have the crib to myself and to just be able to do the things that I used to do before they came. Smoke weed in the house, and fuck my lady with the bedroom door open while she got as loud as she wanted to.

My mother is a police officer, and my father is a truck driver. They both work long, crazy hours, so they help me with the girls as much as they can, but I don't hold it against them that they work a lot. They're setting themselves up for retirement. Since I'm my own boss, my schedule is flexible, so between the girls going to school, my parents, and their paternal grandfather, I have help. Sometimes, I let them hang out at the shop with me.

Their father, Mike, has been in prison for the past four years, and he has five more to go. His mother isn't shit, and she's not in his life or the girls' lives, but his father is the real MVP. When Charles' wife got addicted to drugs when Mike was small, Charles put her out and raised his four kids as a single father. Even when Mike chose to go the wrong route and live a life that his father didn't approve of, his father stuck by his side, and he did a lot for the girls. He took them fishing, gave them money every week, even if it was only $20, and called them every two or three days. They don't like spending the night at his house because he doesn't have cable, and they say it's boring, but Charles is an old school grandfather, and I'm glad the girls have him.

They talk to their father twice a week, but they haven't been to visit him in about six months. Their mother's death already traumatized them, and I just didn't like the idea of dragging the girls to a prison monthly. Maybe me not taking them more often was what was adding to some of the damage. Maybe they needed their father. To look him in the face and talk to him. Most days, I didn't know what was right or wrong. I just did whatever I felt was right and prayed that it wouldn't add to their trauma.

I pulled up at the restaurant that Tiesha wanted to eat at and found a parking space. She'd been with me long enough to know to stay put when I got out of the car. I walked around to her side and opened the door for her. We walked hand in hand to the entrance, and I opened the door so she could walk through it. I had made reservations, so after I gave the hostess my name, we were seated in less than five minutes. On the way to our booth, I let Tiesha walk in front of me, and my eyes were focused on her ass in the black and white skirt she wore that was ankle length but had a high split on the right side, showing enough thigh to make a nigga fantasize about what I wanted to do to her later.

Once we were seated, there was no need to look over the menu, because we both knew what we wanted. The waitress came over to the table, and I recognized her immediately. She was the woman that I'd tatted the butterflies on the day before. Shorty was pretty, but I saw pretty women every day. That shit didn't move me or tempt me to cheat on Tiesha, but there was something about her. Maybe it was the way her face lit up when her son face timed her.

Maybe I had a soft spot for her because she had kids around the same age as my nieces.

She smiled at me and Tiesha and asked us what we wanted to drink. The smile was all she gave me. She didn't mention the day before or the tattoo, and I could appreciate that. Tiesha knew I tattooed a lot of women, but she wasn't really the jealous type. I'd never given her a reason to feel like I was doing dirt, and I believed that she trusted me. She wasn't so trusting, however that she couldn't pick up on when a woman was flirting with me, and that shit would set her off bad. So, I was glad that shorty kept it all the way professional. When she walked off, I looked across the table at Tiesha.

"You think you can get two or three days off next month? How much PTO you got? I want to take the girls to Universal Studios."

Tiesha's brows hiked up. "Umm, I have like forty hours, but I was trying to save my days for an adult vacation. I don't want to use three days of my time to do something that's not fun to me. Universal Studios is not my idea of a vacation." The slight scowl on her face rubbed me the wrong way, and at that point, I didn't give a damn about possibly overreacting.

"What's good, yo? Because anytime I try to include you in something with the girls, you look at me like I called you out of your name. You don't fuck with my nieces like that?" my nostrils flared as I waited for her answer because I was pissed.

Tiesha's head jerked back, and she had the nerve to look shocked. "Saying I don't fuck with them is a little dramatic. You don't even have to act like that. I'm just being honest, Houston. My birthday is coming up, and I want to take four days off for that. I want to go on vacation where I can smoke hookah, get pissy drunk, go to the club, and live life. I'm sorry if my idea of a good vacation isn't walking around an amusement park all day. I don't have kids, Houston."

"Tell me how you really feel," I glared at her. "Put the shit on the table. How do you feel about me raising my nieces?"

Tiesha shifted nervously in the booth, and her eyes darted around the room for a few moments before her orbs landed back on my face. "I'm not sure why you're acting all upset, but if you want me to keep it real with you, Houston, I will. Neither one of us have kids, and I was looking forward to us moving in together and having a baby in the next two or three years. I'm twenty-four, so I'm not a child, but I'm not old as hell either.

For just a little while, I want to sleep in when I don't have to work. I enjoy not having anyone else to be responsible for. I like going to the club and being free to come and go as I please. Your nieces are your family, and I love how you love them, but I didn't sign up to become an insta parent. Getting up early to get them ready for school, taking boring vacations, not being able to come and go as we please, that's not the life I wanted for us right now, or I would have gotten pregnant."

I knew it. I already knew that's how she felt, so I wasn't shocked at all. I'd be lying if I said I wasn't disappointed though. "This isn't the life that you want right now, so why are you with me?"

Tiesha kissed her teeth and shook her head. "Because I love you. Why do you think? But we're in a relationship, Houston. Again, I know those are your nieces, but you didn't discuss anything with me. I just looked up one day, and they were there. You didn't ask me how I felt then, so I'm a little shocked that you're asking me now."

My left leg was bouncing anxiously underneath the table. I was trying to keep my composure, but Tiesha had me fucked up. I'm far from an emotional nigga, but the things she was saying was pissing me off. The more she talked, the madder I became.

"I didn't discuss shit with you?" I asked in a low tone, laced with venom. "I didn't know my sister was going to off herself. I'm sorry that shit didn't come with notice. I did what I had to for my family, and as my girl, I felt you would have understood and supported me."

Shorty came to the table with our drinks, so

Tiesha refrained from replying right away. When ole girl walked away, Tiesha sipped from her glass of wine before licking her lip and continuing. "This is why I never said anything. I didn't want you to be mad, but how can you say I don't support you? Who keeps the girls' hair braided? Who cooks for y'all multiple times a week? I'm just speaking my truth. I'm not even ready for my own child, so for you to wake up one day and have two kids, that was a lot for me."

I stared at Tiesha. If that was her truth, there wasn't a thing I could do about it. She didn't have to be happy about me getting custody of my nieces. She didn't have to support me either, but all my suspicions had been confirmed. Tiesha wasn't feeling the fact that I had taken my nieces in, and I wasn't going to beg her to accept them. I loved her, but if I had to choose, it would be a no-brainer.

"My nieces aren't going anywhere, so I guess I'll let you be free. You don't want a nigga with kids, go find one," I stated adamantly, and her mouth fell open.

"I know you're not dismissing me, Houston. You're breaking up with me because I'm honest? That's some bullshit. I'm wrong for feeling like your parents should be the one to take them in?"

My upper lip curled into a snarl. "My parents don't have to take in shit because I wanted my nieces. I'm sorry if that's not the life you want, and I'm giving you permission to go be free. Since they came, you don't want to live with a nigga, you don't spend the night, and you don't want to go on vacations with us. Your actions speak volumes, so that's what it is then. My nieces aren't leaving my house until they're well over the age of eighteen, but you can get the fuck on now."

Tiesha's eyes widened. "Wow, Houston. How did our date night turn into this?"

"Because I get sick of trying to include you in shit, and you act like you'd rather be anywhere in the world than with me and my nieces. They aren't going anywhere, Tiesha. My sister already left them. Their father isn't around. I'm not going to abandon them because you don't like the fact that I took them in."

"And we have to do this now? On our date?"

"Ain't no date, ma. I'm ready to go," I stated in a flat tone. The waitress came over with the food, and I pulled out my wallet. "I need to-go boxes and the check."

I didn't even want to wait for her to come back with the tab. I just took two $100 bills out of my wallet and placed them on the table. She scurried off to get the takeout boxes, and Teisha was staring at me with a slacked jaw. The meal and two drinks probably weren't more than $140, but she could keep the change.

"I absolutely can't believe this. So, you're breaking up with me?"

I scoffed at her. "Don't say the shit like me leaving you is some impossible shit. I love you. I saw a future with you, but if you can't get with my nieces being around, there will never be an us. I gave you a year to get used to the shit. I could peep from day one that you didn't like it, but this is what I was trying to avoid."

Tears filled Tiesha's eyes. Now, she was about to play the victim. "I don't even want to ride back with you. I'll get an Uber."

"Say less," I replied as the waitress came back with the takeout trays. My appetite was gone, but I was taking my food since I paid for it. Tiesha could do what she wanted with hers.

She was still sitting there after I raked the food from my plate into the black, plastic, container , so I stood up and headed for the exit. She had me fucked up.

* * *

After my fucked up date, I went home, smoked a blunt, listened to music, and zoned out while drinking cognac. I passed out after the fifth shot of liquor, and I didn't get back up until the next day when the cleaning lady rang the doorbell and woke me up. While she cleaned, I started some laundry and cooked breakfast. I couldn't help but think about the night before with Tiesha, but I refused to dwell on that shit.

I was faithful to her, I saw a future with her, and I loved her. But sometimes, shit wasn't meant to be. I gave her an adequate amount of time to get used to the fact that my nieces were now an intricate part of my life. If she wasn't with the shit after a year, she'd never be with it, and I had to go on with my life. I didn't want to be in a foul mood. I didn't want the end of the relationship to put me in a bad headspace, but I was cranky as shit.

Before I took the girls in, I had a carefree life with minimal responsibilities. Taking in two kids was a big adjustment. Tiesha had a right to feel how she felt, but I had made my choice. I was single again, and it was what it was. I took a shower and got dressed after I ate breakfast. By that time, the cleaning lady was done, and I paid her and left to go pick up my nieces.

My parents live in a house ten miles from me that they paid off a year ago. They both have good jobs and have been in their professions since I was around ten. They're both close to retirement, and my sister's death hit them hard. My mom took three weeks off of work, and in the midst of her grief, she had to be there for Omi and Terrionna. She wasn't ready to retire just yet, so I offered to take the girls in, and I didn't regret it. If Tiesha couldn't get with it, then she just wasn't the girl for me. A lot of people were shocked that a man as young as me wanted the responsibility of two kids that I didn't make. It really makes me feel like I'm built different than most people because taking them in wasn't even something that I had to think hard about.

Yeah, my life changed a lot, but going to the club every weekend, being able to smoke in my house whenever I wanted to, hanging out until four in the morning, all that was cool, but it didn't hold enough weight for me not to get my nieces.

My sister was two years younger than me, and we'd been thick as thieves since she was about four. We rarely argued, and we were always getting into trouble together. I was the overprotective big brother, and when she started dating, I didn't like that shit. I was on Mike's ass hard because I could tell she really liked him, and that nigga took her through hell. During the six years that they were together, I beat his ass twice.

When they finally broke up for good, Bria was sick. She was barely eating. She stopped going out with friends or getting her hair done. She completely let herself go, and she got fired from her job for missing too many days. I hated to see her so heartbroken, so I helped her in whatever way I could. I was just getting my tattoo shop open, but I was making good money, and I helped her with her bills and expenses for the girls.

After about four months, I thought Bria was getting better. I thought she was finally getting over the end of her relationship. She had started a new job, and the last time I was around her, she was smiling and appeared happy. Two days after that though, Omi called my mother one morning hysterical, saying that her mother wouldn't wake up. My mom went over there, and Bria was dead. She had taken something the night before, got in her bed, and died in her sleep. Omi was the one to find her, and I knew she'd never forget that shit.

Me, my parents, and Bria's kids had gone through it, and Tiesha had the nerve to act like our tragedy inconvenienced her. Fuck her, and I put that on everything I love. When I arrived at my parents' house, I smiled at my father playing basketball in the driveway with Omi and Terrionna. My parents have been together for over thirty years, and my pops is that nigga. The way he provided for us and the way he loves my mom is top tier. He was my role model for sure, and I enjoyed making him proud.

I caught a gun charge at nineteen, and my parents were disappointed, but my father also understood where I was coming from. I never sold drugs, but I got into smoking weed and hanging out in the hood with my homies when I was fourteen. I learned quickly that everyone from young, black men to middle-aged women needed to be out here toting because niggas were crazy for real. I'm quiet and keep to myself. I never really had beef with anyone, but there are those people that think quiet niggas are pussy, so I had to show them.

I don't carry a gun for ignorant niggas because my hands work. But if anyone thought they would ever get the pleasure of jumping me, robbing me, or anything along those lines, they were going to see just how fast I put them in the dirt. My dad and I have always been close, and when I broke it down to him like that, he understood. When I decided I wanted my own tattoo shop, I took a job in a warehouse to make it happen. I didn't want to go to college, but I lived at home with my parents for a year and stacked my money. When that year was up, I had $24,000, and my father went to his bank and took out a loan for $40,000.

I got my shop, continued to live at home for another six months, and then I got my own apartment. I did pretty good at first, but my breakthrough happened when one of my classmates got drafted to the Miami Heat. Before he left to go to Miami, I did a tattoo for him that was the best work I'd ever done. His teammates saw it and went crazy, and even though there are many talented tattoo artists in

Miami, two of them asked me to fly down and do a tat for them. They paid for my flight, and I did the tattoos in one of their homes.

After I posted the pics to Instagram and Facebook, I blew up from there. As of right now, I'm booked for the next five months. I've even had rappers and athletes pay me as much as $2,000 to leave my whole day free and come through to tat them for hours. I might tat for an hour, they'll take a thirty minute break, then we'll get back to it for another hour or so. I loved my job, and I loved being able to live a comfortable life and provide for my nieces by doing something that I enjoyed. I hated every moment of working in that warehouse, but I knew that it was only temporary and necessary if I wanted to make my dreams come true.

I got out of the car, and Terrionna ran over to me and wrapped her arms around my legs. "Hey, Uncle Houston. I missed you."

I chuckled. "I was only gone for half a day. You must want something. What's good?"

She looked up at me and laughed because she knew I'd called her out. "I just want to stop by the mall on the way home and go into the Leggo store."

"We can do that, shawty."

She beamed up at me before running off, and I looked over at Omi. She wasn't speaking to a nigga, but it was cool. The first day kind of hurt my feelings.

I won't lie. But I knew she'd get over it. I was trying to help Omi, and I had come to the conclusion that babying her and not holding her accountable for her actions would only hurt her in the long run.

"I don't go back on the road until tomorrow." My father walked towards me. "You can leave them for another night if you want. You working today?"

"I'm going in, in a few hours. I was going to spend some time with them before I headed to work. You haven't been home in eight days, and I know ma wants to spend some time with you."

My dad gave a slight nod. "Long as you know, they're always good over here. How was your date?"

I leaned up against my car as I watched Omi and Terrionna continue to play without my father. "A bust. We broke up. She's not really feeling the fact that I have the girls, and they're not going anywhere, so..."

"So fuck her," my father stated calmly. "I'm sure it was a big adjustment for her. I can't even sit up here and act like she's wrong for not feeling how she feels, but family is family. Whether we signed up for this or not, Bria is gone. There's no way in hell we wouldn't be here for her kids.

I just put a new roof on this house, and your mother is two years away from being able to get her pension. Taking the girls in full-time would have been a challenge, and the fact that you stepped up to the plate is admirable because most men your age wouldn't have done it. Tiesha isn't a bad person, but she's not the one for you, and I damn sure hope you don't feel bad about it being over."

"Not at all," I replied. "When I took the girls in, life changed real fast, but not in a bad way. Omi gives me a run for my damn money, but I wouldn't have it any other way. I love Tiesha, but she's not the end all be all. I wish her the best."

"Straight like that."

Me and my father conversed for another twenty minutes or so before I left to take the girls to the mall. In the car, Terrionna asked me the same question that my father had. "How was your date? Did you have fun? Did you bring me back food?"

I chuckled and looked up in the rearview mirror. "No, I didn't bring you food because you were here and not home. And the date was aight. Me and Tiesha broke up, so she won't be at the house anymore."

I watched Terrionna's face crumple. "Oh no. Are you going to be sad? When mommy and daddy broke up, mommy was sad. She cried all the time." Terrionna's voice was small, and I swallowed down a lump that had formed in my throat.

"Nah, Baby Girl. I'm not sad. Break-ups happen sometimes. It will be okay." I reassured her. While watching her, I saw Omi shrug passively.

"She didn't like us anyway."

I gritted my back teeth together as I turned and looked over my shoulder at her. "Why you say that?"

Omi shrugged, avoiding eye contact. "She just didn't. Sometimes, she acted like we got on her nerves."

I tried to make it a habit not to call women out of their names in front of my nieces, so it took a lot for me to remain respectful. I was pissed at the fact that Tiesha had ever made them feel that way. I thought I was the only one that picked up on that vibe. I had no clue that the kids could feel it, and I felt that was another area that I dropped the ball in.

"Well, you don't have to worry about that anymore. Aight?"

I stared at Omi until she stopped being stubborn and looked over at me. She nodded and gave me a small smile.

Chapter Five

CYPHER

I watched patiently in the shoe store as Qori and Quentin looked over the sneakers. I knew it would take them forever to decide which ones they wanted, and I knew they'd try to talk me out of only getting them two pairs each. I buy the boys' sneakers two at a time every two to three months. Purchasing four pairs of sneakers at once is never cheap, but I had worked some overtime, and I had an extra $200 to spare. I was going to charge the sneakers on my credit card then turn around and pay $200 on the card. When I got my next check, I'd go ahead and pay it off. I tried to keep a nice balance on my credit card at all times in the event of an emergency. My available credit was $18,000, and it was hard sometimes not to splurge on myself with that money, but I knew I had to be responsible.

My period had to be coming because I was

emotional out of nowhere. I got teary eyed in the shower that morning, and I had been feeling down in the dumps all day, and I really didn't even know why. Maybe I did. After I got the boys sneakers, a few new outfits, filled my gas tank up, and bought household supplies for the apartment, my entire check would be gone, and I'd be back hustling at the restaurant just to have pocket money. It seemed as if all I did was work and stress money, and the shit was getting old and mundane. I had fun on my birthday, and now it was back to the real world, knowing it would be a long time before I could treat myself again.

I looked up and did a double take as I noticed my cousin, Khelisi, and her boyfriend Shaiheem coming in the store. I hadn't seen her in forever, and her stomach was huge. We locked eyes, and a huge smile covered her face as she rushed over to me.

"Cypher," she squealed. "Where are the boys?" she looked around until she spotted them, and her eyes widened. "Oh my gosh, they are so big! How have you been?"

Khelisi was mature for her age. Always had been, but there was an age difference with us, so we were never super close as far as hanging out together. She had her friends, and I had mine, but we would always talk when we saw each other.

"I've been good. Congratulations," I smiled and

rubbed her belly. "You look like you are about to pop! When are you due?"

Khelisi rolled her eyes and groaned as her handsome, green eyed boyfriend came over and stood by her side. "Girl, not for another three weeks. I want this little boy out of me, do you hear me?"

"Imagine there being two hims in there," I giggled. "I didn't get an invite to the baby shower?" I lifted an eyebrow, and she shook her head.

"I didn't have one. Well, let me take that back. I didn't plan one. My co-workers surprised me with one, but I didn't have one and invite people. I've just been weird during this pregnancy. I didn't do a gender reveal or anything. I just work and sit in the house with my man."

"There's nothing wrong with that at all. I want to know the moment you push him out. I'm definitely going to get him something."

"I want us to do lunch soon. I know you're older than me, but I'm in a relationship with a baby on the way, and I live with my man. That ratchet hanging out in the streets shit isn't my thing anymore. I don't need a lot of people around me, but the ones I do have around me need to be on the same page as me. I've outgrown some people since I got pregnant, and that's okay."

"It absolutely is. Just call me. I work two jobs, so

I'm stretched thin most of the time, but I do get some free time here and there."

"Bet." Khelisi smiled as the boys ran over to me with the shoes they wanted. "They are so freaking cute. I know I've missed mad birthdays, and I'm going to do better. Whatever shoes they get, I'm paying for."

My brows shot up. "Khelisi, you really don't have to do that. Honestly. I appreciate it, but tha—"

She waved me off. "I just got a raise, and my man pays all the bills. He will barely even let me buy groceries for the house. I'm not taking no for an answer. Stop being stubborn and blocking your blessings."

She was right. "Say less." I chuckled.

Khelisi and I talked while the boys tried on their shoes, and then she paid for them as promised. I told her I'd call her in the next few days so we could set up a time to do lunch, and though I was super grateful that she had bought the boys' shoes, the sadness that I had been feeling all day outweighed my joy. Seeing her with her man, glowing, and doing well in life made me happy for her but sad for myself at the same time.

It was hard not to be bitter when watching everyone else have the things you wanted. All I wanted was a man that wanted a family. I didn't want a nigga that was always in the streets, toting guns and getting in trouble. I wanted a family-oriented man that knew how to provide, but I would still work and bring something to the table. I didn't have to be a stay at home mom, but I wanted a man that knew how to lead and take care of his family. Why was that so much to ask for? I wanted my boys to grow up in a two-parent home the same way I did but with each passing year, I was faced with the sad reality that I just might have to raise them alone.

Since Khelisi bought their shoes, I was able to buy them more outfits than I had originally planned on. I also picked up a gift for Kimbella's husband's nephew. She was taking the boys to their birthday party later, and I wasn't going to let them show up empty handed. When we left the mall, we went home, and the boys took a shower and changed into a new outfit and their new shoes. They played the game while they waited on Kimbella to come, and I began deep cleaning the apartment.

It was my last full day off for a while, and I needed to get a lot of things done. Laundry being the main one. Kimbella arrived, and I gave the boys knowing looks. "I better not get one bad report. I mean it. Go to that party and act like you have some home training. Don't make me pull up with my belt."

They laughed, but I was serious. As soon as they left, I got back to cleaning and out of nowhere, tears filled my eyes. "Ughhh! What is wrong with you today, bitch?" I groaned. I hated being sad and in my feelings.

I should be used to being single. I should be used to being alone and not getting dick on a regular basis, but it still hurt sometimes.

"I definitely don't want you to lower your standards. You don't have to rush it, but don't be closed off either. The right one will come along."

Kimbella's words ran through my mind as I washed dishes. Going out alone made me feel pathetic, but I knew I had to get out of that. I had to start being comfortable with my own company and stop acting as if I couldn't be fully happy unless I had a man in my face. I'd rather raise the boys alone than to have them around dysfunctional bullshit. Relationships didn't always equate to happy.

An hour later, my apartment was spotless, and I had decided to take myself out on a date. I took a shower, exfoliated my skin, and gave myself a facial. After moisturizing my body, I gave my face a light beat, flat ironed my hair, and put on a purple, white, and green print max dress that was so long it swept the floor when I walked. I felt pretty as I sprayed on some perfume and then added gold accessories. I knew the boys would be gone for another hour or two, and that gave me enough time to sit down in a nice restaurant and treat myself to a nice meal. I might even stop at the store and buy myself some flowers on the way home. I deserved it.

* * *

The next day, I picked the boys up from school and went to get an oil change. I didn't want to be spending $100 on that, but it was necessary. I had been ignoring the notification on my dash for the past three weeks. I thought I could get it done after I dropped the boys off at practice, but practice was canceled due to rain. We were now sitting in the waiting area, and it was taking everything in me not to scream. Qori was being overly obnoxious and getting a kick out of annoying his brother. They had been bickering for the past ten minutes, and I was over it.

"Will you freakin' stop?!" I hissed at Qori. "What is wrong with you? Do I need to take that iPad? He's asked you five times to leave him alone. Now leave him alone!" I whispered harshly.

Qori hates being chastised, and he balled his face up tight while his chest heaved up and down. I cocked my head to the side.

"You know you can't beat me, right? I suggest you stop looking at me like that before I hurt your feelings."

"Be easy, butterflies."

My head snapped in the direction of that sexy ass tone, and my clit thumped as my eyes landed on Houston. I swore that man only got finer each time that I saw him. When I saw him at the restaurant the other night on a date, the surge of jealousy that shot through my body confused the hell out of me. I didn't know that man from a can of paint, but on that night, I would have paid money to go home with him and ride his face. I viewed the woman that he was out with as the luckiest woman in the world, but that went away when I saw her alone at the table with tears in her eyes after he left.

I wasn't sure what had happened, but Houston came across as so sweet. I couldn't see him possessing fuck boy qualities, but we don't see a lot of these men possessing those qualities until it's too late. Now, here he was standing in front of me looking real damn delicious, and I was irritated that the Universe kept tempting me. I had never seen this man in person before he did my tattoo and now, I'd seen him three times in one week. Tuh.

I gave him a sheepish grin. "These kids are irritating the heck out of me. Cypher. My name is Cypher."

"Cypher. I like that name. When you booked your appointment, I wasn't sure if that was your real name." He diverted his attention towards the boys. "I heard y'all be getting it in on the field. When is your next game? I might stop by and bring my nieces."

My heart fell into my ass, and I swallowed hard. So, I would be around him yet again. What was going on? Quentin spoke up as I continued to stare up at Houston. "Wednesday at four. We play at the rec center on Glennwood."

"Bet. I'll slide through." He gave the boys a nod and winked at me before walking off.

I had to steady my damn breathing. I had already told the boys it might not be possible for me to make every game, but I was off on Wednesday and had already told them I'd be there. I know we have to teach our kids to be independent, but I never wanted them to play in a game where there wasn't at least *one* person in the stands rooting for them. Between me, my parents, Kimbella, and her husband, we generally made it happen. But hearing Houston say he was going to come check them out made my heart swell, and I knew the boys liked it too because they both grinned when he said he was coming.

Five minutes later, my name was being called, and I went to the front desk to pay and get my keys. The guy behind the counter gave me the sheet that detailed what he'd done and slid me the keys. "Have a nice day. Come back and see us soon. You're almost due for a tire rotation."

"Um, okay. Is the price on the paper?" I scanned it until I found what I was looking for.

"Oh, um, I thought you knew. It's already been paid for. You're set."

I raised one brow and looked around, but I didn't see any signs of Houston. "Oh okay. Thank you."

My heart raced as I picked the keys up and left. First, Khelisi bought the boys some shoes, and Houston paid for my oil change. I had been feeling so down and discouraged lately that I guess God was just sending me random blessings, and I sure appreciated them. If it's one thing I do, it's try. And that's what makes it so frustrating. I work two jobs, so I can't get food stamps. I work hard just to take care of me and my boys, and I often cry because I mostly do it alone. Kimbella buys them things, and so do my parents, but Qori and Quentin and my bills are my responsibility. The only person that was obligated to help me was Nick, but it would be a cold day in hell before that happened.

I bit back a smile as I headed for the exit. Thank God for small miracles.

Chapter Six

HOUSTON

I arrived at the rec center and got out of the car. Omi and Terrionna were on my heels as we headed for the gate that led to the football field. I paid for three tickets and was let through. I observed that there was a nice lil' turn out, but the bleachers weren't so full that I couldn't easily spot Cypher. I was glad to support the kids as a whole because I knew what we spent on tickets went back into the rec center. I didn't know a thing about Cypher. I didn't know if she was married, single, dating multiple men, or what. I had no clue, but me coming to see the kids play wasn't about me pushing up on her.

I had done two tattoos earlier, and I didn't have any more appointments until later in the night, so this was also a chance to chill with my nieces. Since I would be at the shop until around two in the morning, my mom was going to come to the house and stay with them until I got in. She had to be at work at five AM anyway, and she would just get dressed and ready to go from there. I have a guest bedroom that she always stays in when she spends the night.

Cypher was sitting alone dressed in black and white leggings and a matching top with white sneakers. Her hair was pulled back in a low bun and diamond studs decorated her ears. Shorty was something nice to look at, and as a man, I was looking. Men are different from women in the sense that when we get out of a relationship, we don't need time to heal or be alone. There was no time restraint on getting the next woman in bed, but I for sure was going to take a break from relationships for a moment.

Cypher smiled at me and my nieces as we climbed the stairs. "Anyone sitting here?" I asked her.

"Nope. I'm here alone."

"This is my niece Ominique, and this is my other niece Terrionna. This is Ms. Cypher."

"I love those names." Cypher's smile grew wider as she beamed at my nieces.

They thanked her and hit me up for money for the concession stand. I chuckled. "The game hasn't even started yet." After fishing some cash from my pocket, I handed them the bills, and they took off.

"I hope I'm not stepping on anyone's toes," I

looked over at Cypher. "I wanted to come out and support the kids. I'm not sure if you have a man or if their father is around or what."

"I'm as single as they come, and their bastard of a father doesn't even know they play football. You're good. I appreciate you coming out. The boys liked knowing that someone outside of family was going to come see them play."

"Anytime. How long you been single?"

"A very long time," she chuckled. "I've dated since me and their father broke up when I was pregnant, but I haven't been in a relationship, and my kids are eight. That says a lot," she shook her head. "And I want to say it's by choice. I mean, when I see that a guy isn't it for me, I move on. I'm not desperate to have a man in my life, so I'm comfortable with being alone, but it does suck sometimes. Just being honest." She shrugged passively. "It's whatever, though. I don't want my kids around dysfunction, so if it isn't right, I can't do it."

"I feel you on that."

"What about you? Are you single? I promised myself I wouldn't be nosey and speak on you and ole girl that night you left her at the restaurant, but..." her voice trailed off.

"I became single as of that night. We were together for two years, and everything was good up until a year ago when I got my nieces. It came out of nowhere and was unexpected, so I can understand that it would take some time for her to get used to. But shorty wasn't feeling me having custody of them. She's not ready for kids, and I brought two of them home out of the blue. I didn't ask her to get up in the mornings and get them ready for school or any of that, but me doing so bothered her. She claimed we'd wake her up making noise, and she couldn't get back to sleep. She doesn't want to take vacations with us or deal with the inconvenience of me not being able to come and go as I please."

"Wow."

"Yeah, so that's that. My nieces are always going to come first, and if a woman can't deal with that, she's free to go."

"I was watching this documentary where a man killed his wife, and his new girlfriend didn't want kids, so he killed the kids too. He just wanted to be able to start over and live a new life with this woman, and I was floored. There are some sick and twisted people in this world. I don't care how lonely I ever get. If a man doesn't accept those twins, he can get the hell out of my face."

"Straight like that."

"Oh," her eyes widened as if she'd just remembered something. "Thank you so much for paying for my oil change the other day. You didn't have to. Thank you."

"It's nothing. Consider it a late birthday present."

"Thanks. Prepare to be embarrassed by me because I'm that mom. I scream at the top of my lungs and do the most once the game starts. I work two jobs, and I can't make every game, so the ones that I can attend, I have to be extra as hell."

"Do you, mama. No apologies necessary."

I thought about the fact that she was a single mother and she worked two jobs. From what I knew of her, Cypher had her head on straight, and she was a damn good mother. I had been out of the dating loop for two years, and I knew I wouldn't have a problem diving back in. I didn't want to waste her time. I had no intentions of leading her on or any of that, but maybe once in a while, I could take her out on a date just to help her relax and get her mind off things. I had no desire to dog her out or do her dirty, but I wasn't out here trying to fall in love either.

"So listen," I started as the teams ran out on the field. "I'm fresh out of a relationship like I just said, so I'm not trying to rush into anything. I also know your time is limited because of work and the boys, but could I maybe take you out sometime? Just two adults hanging out. No pressure."

A small smile graced her face. "I'd like that."

I pulled out my phone and locked her number in just as my nieces were coming back with all kinds of food and snacks. Hot dogs, nachos, hot pickles, candy, sodas.

"Damn. Y'all didn't even ask me if I wanted anything."

Terrionna smiled wide, showing off the wide space in her mouth due to losing two teeth. "I got you nachos."

"I got you a soda," Omi stated, and I smiled.

"Oh, so y'all do love a nigga."

The game started, and for the kids to be so young, it was intense if you asked me. Cypher's sons were nice on the field, and I knew that if they stuck with it and continued to play, they'd be nothing short of amazing. When a kid fell trying to tackle Quentin, and lil' man jumped over the kid's body and ran as fast as his little legs would carry him and scored a touchdown, the crowd went crazy. Even my nieces were into the game, and Terrionna expressed wanting to be a cheerleader.

I was glad I brought them out. When the game was over, I made it my business to stay and tell the kids what a good job they had done. As soon as they approached their mother, I gave them high fives. "Y'all didn't tell me y'all were that nice. Your touchdowns were the reason your team won. Good ass job."

The boys and Cypher beamed with pride. I said my goodbyes and went to drop my nieces off, so I could get to the shop. I was going to have to tread lightly with Ms. Cypher. She deserved a real nigga that would treat her nice, spoil her a lil' bit, and give her some D that made her soul leave her body, but the question was if she'd be able to handle all that without falling in love.

* * *

I pulled from the blunt and passed it to Zeke. It was a little after midnight, and I was still at the shop. Zeke came through, and we smoked a blunt. My last client was gone, and I was just cleaning up in preparation to leave. My next appointment was the following day at 1 PM, so I knew I could take the girls to school, work out, shower, and get a short nap in before work.

"You know Tiesha been crying to Cresha and shit," Zeke's voice was strained due to the weed smoke that he was holding in his lungs.

We've been friends for the past fifteen years, so when me and Tiesha got together, we went on a few double dates with Zeke and his girl Cresha. They've been together for five years.

"I really don't give a fuck," I replied dryly. "Her tears don't mean shit to me. If my nieces haven't grown on her in a year, then they probably never will. I'm not staying with a broad that doesn't like the fact that I have custody of my sister's kids. That broad really asked me why my parents didn't take them in."

"You know I don't blame you. One of my homies grew up in foster care because his moms went to prison when he was seven, and no one in his family wanted to take him in. You know how that made that nigga feel? To know that out of all his flesh and blood, they'd rather let a stranger raise him than take him in? When his mom got out when he was ten, she got him back, but to this day, he refuses to fuck with his family. He won't do holidays or anything. You did what family is supposed to do, and if she can't respect that, fuck her."

"She's going to go around and play victim though and make it look like I overreacted and did her wrong. Omi even said she could tell that Tiesha didn't like them. You know how that made me feel, bro? This woman held me while I cried over my sister. She knew how bad that shit hurt me, and she wants me to do my sister's kids dirty?" I was getting heated just thinking about it.

"Aye, Bria was your sister, but I've been around her countless times, and you know we had a cool lil' friendship too. Her doing what she did messed me up, so I can only imagine how you feel. Tiesha will be aight. I told Cresha to stop even talking to me about her goofy ass. She got what she deserved."

"Talking about Universal Studios isn't her idea of a

fun vacation. I was going to surprise her with a birthday trip to Bali, but she missed out on that shit, and I saved hella money, so it's a win-win for me. I didn't want our life to be all about my nieces. I was going to do a family trip and a trip with just me and Tiesha. Her loss. I'm good on it."

"Now you can get some new pussy, nigga. I swear, since Cresha left my ass for cheating three years ago and took me back, I've been on my best behavior, but I'm fiending for some new pussy bad as hell. When I'm around another woman, I hear that shit calling me. I think I'm losing my mind." I laughed as he passed the blunt back to me. "I'm dead ass, bro. Cresha's pussy is damn good, but I want something new so bad, my nigga. At least your ass can go dip in something new now."

"Being faithful wasn't even a problem for me. It would have been mad easy to be a dog ass nigga though. Do you know how many women practically beg to have sex with me? I made turning down pussy a sport, and shorty gave all that up because I'm a loyal nigga. She wanted me to be loyal to her but not my nieces. I don't get the logic." I was tired of talking about Tiesha's ass.

Zeke sat and peered off into space as if he was in deep thought. "I've been thinking about starting a big ass argument and leaving the house for five or six days, so I can go hit something new."

"Nigga," I kissed my teeth. "I wouldn't advise you to do that dumb shit. Last time Cresha left you, you were sick as fuck. I got tired of hearing you cry. Don't do that shit."

Zeke turned his head slowly and looked at me. "Nigga, fuck you."

I laughed and grabbed my keys before cutting off the light and walking towards the front. If I had it my way, this would be my last time ever talking about Tiesha and how she didn't like the fact that I was raising my nieces. I loved her, but I had too much pride to be heartbroken over a grimy female, and to me, that's what Tiesha was. She showed me her character, and it was one that I didn't fuck with. So, I was good on her. Chapter closed.

Chapter Seven

CYPHER

"Has he called yet?" Kimbella asked as I stood at her stove stirring the macaroni and cheese I had poured into a pan.

It had been three days since I gave Houston my number, and it was a rare day that I had an entire Saturday off. I was glad to have the whole weekend off but kind of perturbed. I worked most Saturdays and always left with no less than $300 in tips. Linda had given me the weekend off, and I couldn't help but to think the bitch was purposely messing with my hours because she knew I didn't like her, but it was cool. I'd just pick up some extra hours at the call center on Tuesday.

"No, and this is the second time you've asked me that. I'm anxious enough. Don't keep asking me about that man."

Kimbella's sister was pregnant, and Kimbella was

hosting the gender reveal. Her husband was outside on the grill, and we were in the kitchen making the sides. Guests weren't due to arrive for another thirty minutes. Qori and Quentin were outside playing with some of the kids in Kimbella's family and her neighbor's kids.

Kimbella held her up hands in surrender. "I want him to call as bad as you do. Didn't I tell you that you deserve a good ass man with some good D? I want that for you real bad, friend."

I smiled. "Shit, I want it for myself. I don't mind a man that has kids because duh, I have two. I just didn't want to deal with baby mama drama. Seeing how he is with his nieces and the fact that he's raising them on his own, do you know how moist that made my panties? That act right there has me ready to bust it open for him, but then he paid for my oil change too, and didn't even ask for my number afterwards? Yeah, he's too toxic, and I should be running, but I want that," I admitted.

"And I want you to have it," Kimbella chimed in, and I erupted into laughter. "I'm serious, friend. And stop all that he's probably toxic and all that other BS. Get some dick. Go on dates. Have fun. Who cares what else he has going on? As long as he doesn't put his hands on you or disrespect you, just worry about how he treats you when he's with you. Don't be so quick to fall in love. Get your rocks off, and don't let that man stress you."

"When you're right, you're right." I slid the pan of macaroni and cheese into the oven. "You know it's hard for a lot of women to just keep their head in it. A few deep strokes and some good game, and our hearts get activated. I really don't have the time or the head-space to worry about what a man is doing though. Between my kids and my jobs, I refuse to be trying to keep up with a man. He just got out of a relationship too. I know he's going to be juggling women."

"Just make him use condoms and keep your heart out it, Cypher. Do that, and you'll be good."

My cell phone started ringing, and I saw an unknown number on the screen. "Hello?"

"This Cypher?" that deep voice made my kitty tingle. We had talked the man up!

"Yes, this is Cypher."

"What's good? This is Houston."

"Hi," I replied with a smile as my body temperature rose. Kimbella turned to look at me with her nosey self, and I turned my back, so she wouldn't see me blushing.

"Did I catch you at a bad time? I know you have more jobs than a Mexican."

I laughed. "No, it's not a bad time. It's a rare day that I have both days off from work. I'm at my friend's house helping her cook. She's hosting a gender reveal today." I grabbed a knife and started slicing strawberries.

"You're off from both jobs today? Damn. It probably would have been a good day to take you on a date, but I know it's last minute. Plus, Saturdays usually boom for me, so I'll be in the shop until two or three in the morning."

I hated the sinking in my stomach caused by disappointment. *Take your heart out of it.* "I can imagine Saturdays in a tattoo shop being lit. It's fine. I'm off tomorrow too. I don't normally get a whole weekend off from my part-time job. I hate my manager, and I don't think she cares too much for me, so something is telling me she's trying to be funny with my hours. It's all good though. I can pretty much get all the overtime I want from my full-time job. The bills will get paid regardless."

"I've been working seven days a week for the past few months because I'm taking a week off next month to take my nieces to Universal Studios, but I only have two appointments tomorrow. Maybe we can do dinner around seven."

"Yeah, we can do that."

"That's what it is then. My next appointment is coming in the door. I just wanted to hear your voice since it's been a few days. You can think of a place you want to go tomorrow, and you can text me."

"Okay. I'll do that."

"Later."

I absolutely hated the giddiness that I was feeling. I was too damn old for that. "It's a date?" Kimbella broke into my thoughts. The anxiousness in her tone made me giggle.

"It's a date."

"Yesssss, bitch!"

* * *

I had just pulled up my white, high-waist leggings when Quentin came into my bedroom pouting. For my date with Houston, I was wearing white leggings, with a white, sleeveless, mock neck bodysuit, and black strappy heels. I was going to wear my hair pulled back into a ponytail and do a light beat on my face.

"Ma, can I block dad?" Quentin asked with a scowl on his face, and my brows furrowed.

"Block him for what?"

A lot of people think kids my sons age didn't need cell phones, but I got them phones for their eighth birthday. It was another expense that added to my burdens, but I liked having constant access to my children.

"He called me fussing at me, asking me why I haven't called him and asking me a lot of questions about you."

I counted to ten in my head because I didn't want to spazz. Nick was a low life piece of shit, but I tried real hard to never talk down on him around my kids. I would let them see for themselves the older they got that he wasn't about shit. But he loved testing me, and I didn't appreciate it. Messing with my kids was the fastest way to get on my bad side.

"He's the adult, and you're the child. It's not your job to reach out to him and check up on him, so he shouldn't be fussing at you about anything. And he for sure shouldn't be asking you anything about me. Don't block him though, because that's your father. I'll talk to him."

"Okay. You look pretty. You're going out with Kimbella?"

It felt weird telling my kids I was going out on a date, and I wasn't sure why because I was grown. "No, not with Kimbella, but I'm going to eat with a friend. I'm almost ready to go. Grab your things and get your shoes on. Tell your brother to do the same."

"Okay."

I didn't want to get mad before my date. I didn't want to be in a funk and have Houston picking up on my negative vibes, but this couldn't wait. I grabbed my phone and called Nick's bitch ass. He already knew I was calling to check him because he answered with an attitude.

"Yeah."

"Stop calling my sons getting on them about not calling you. You're supposed to be the parent, even if you don't act like one," I hissed in a low tone. "It's not their job to reach out to you, and you won't fuss at them about it. Don't get blocked from calling their phone. It's not like you help pay the bill."

Nick kissed his teeth. "That's one of the reasons I don't come around. I can't even discipline my own kids without you always having something to say. My sons are your favorite line. Last time I checked, they were my sons too."

"Oh really?" my brows hiked up. "They're your sons too? Because last I checked, you didn't buy one outfit, pair of socks, or draws for them to wear. You haven't spent a dime helping me pay for their football expenses, and you damn sure didn't help with their last birthday. You haven't given my kids a dime in more than a year. You don't make the effort to come see them or reach out to them, and when you do think to call them, you're always trying to fuss at them about some shit. I really want you to leave my kids alone, and I'm not going to keep telling you. We're good without you. You can sign over your rights for all I care."

"I just might do that because I get sick of dealing with your ass, and I don't want to have to do it for the next ten years."

I ended the call and blocked him because I'd given Nick enough of my energy. It used to make me cry that he did my boys how he did them, but I wasn't about to keep crying over that shit. My kids had me, they had my father, and they had Kimbella's husband. There were plenty of men in their lives that taught them things that I couldn't. I didn't think more kids were in the cards for me because I was already thirty-three without a man in sight, and I would never do this to myself again. I'd never get pregnant by a sorry ass man and have to raise my child alone, so if two kids were all it was meant for me to have, then so be it.

I dropped the boys off at my parents' house and drove to the restaurant to meet Houston. I wasn't sure why I was so nervous about seeing him because he was so laid back and chill. For Houston to be so fine, he was very laid back, and I loved that. He didn't seem to have an arrogant bone in his body, while I knew men that didn't look half as good as him that felt they were the prize and should be chased. I didn't care how fine a man was. I wasn't doing the pursuing, but Houston didn't come off like the kind of man that wanted to be chased.

When I arrived at the restaurant, I saw him standing by the door looking real damn good in black jeans and a red sweater with wheat-colored Timbs on his feet. He was the right amount of rugged and sexy.

I checked myself in the visor and got out of the car. I smiled as I approached Houston, and he greeted me with a hug.

"You look nice," he complimented and opened the door for me.

"Thank you. So do you."

We were led to a table, and I wanted a drink bad as hell to keep my nerves at bay. "How was your day?" he asked.

"It's been good. I got a lot done last night as far as preparing for the week, so when I get the boys later and go home, I'm just going to chill out in my bed watching TV and relaxing."

"Where do you work besides the restaurant?"

"A call center that I hate, but it pays the rent and my car note. I can also pick up overtime anytime I'm in a bind and need extra money, so that's another reason why I haven't left. Having two kids is very expensive, and when you don't have help like that, you have to do what you have to do."

"I found out how expensive kids are when I got my nieces. I swear they both hit a growth spurt overnight. They just woke up one day and couldn't fit any of their clothes."

The way Houston's eyes lit up when he talked about the girls made my heart warm. A lot of people would have taken their family in if they had to, but they might not have done so with the genuineness, patience, and kindness that Houston possessed. I could tell he didn't have his nieces out of obligation. He really loved taking care of them.

"If you don't mind me asking, how did your nieces come to live with you?"

"My sister committed suicide."

My breath caught in my throat. "I am so sorry to hear that. Wow, I'm sorry that I asked." Life as a single mother got very hard sometimes. There were days where all I did was cry, and sometimes, death seemed like the easy way out, but the thought of leaving my kids on this earth was one I couldn't bear. I didn't care how tough things got. I felt I owed it to them to stick it out for them, but I wasn't judging Houston's sister at all.

"It's cool. It's life. I think about it every day. There's nothing that talking about it will make me feel that I don't already feel. I don't know what was going through her mind at the time. I do know that she was heartbroken over a bum ass nigga and overwhelmed with being a single parent. I helped her as much as I could, but she was one of those prideful people that liked to act like she was okay when she wasn't, and she hated asking for help. I just wish I had known she was hurting that bad. I would have done whatever I could have for her. I would have taken the girls for a few months, paid her bills, whatever."

I could tell he really meant that, and my heart ached for him and for his sister. She had some beautiful daughters, and she would miss them growing up. "I'm glad they have you. I can tell you do a really good job with them."

"Thanks. I feel the same way about you. Maybe that's why I kind of have a soft spot for you. I see a single mother, and I think of my sister."

"I get it."

The waitress came, and I ordered a strawberry margarita and spinach dip for an appetizer. We went through the usual get to know one another spiel, and I was shocked to learn that I was five years older than him because Houston seemed so mature. By the time dessert came, I was sad that the date was almost over. It was the first date that I'd been on in over a year, and I had a really good time.

"I think getting the tattoo for my birthday activated something in me because all I've been thinking about is another one. I might treat myself sometime soon," I stated.

"We locked in now. You don't have to pay me for a tattoo. Just let me know when you want one, and I'll squeeze you in."

"I don't want you to think that because we're out on a date that I expect you to do things for me. I appreciate the oil change, and I thank you for dinner, but tattoos are how you pay your bills. You don't have to tattoo me for free."

Houston chuckled. "I appreciate the concern, mama, but I'm good on my bills. I'm booked up for months. My shop gets great business, and the other artists in my shop pay me booth rent. I'm a very humble person, but trust me when I say I'm not hurting for money. Doing a free tattoo for you isn't going to send me to the poor house."

He didn't have to tell me twice. As long as he knew that I wasn't expecting anything from him, if he chose to do nice things for me, I damn sure wouldn't refuse it. "As soon as I can decide on what I want and where, I'll let you know."

"You think we should do something with the kids one day? I mean, I don't want to do too much too fast, but the kids might enjoy it."

This man just kept right on tugging at my heartstrings. I hadn't been serious with anyone in a very long time, but I'd never had a guy try to include my kids in anything with me. I'm not the type to have my kids around random men, but as an adult, I could have male friends the same way I had female friends. I wasn't opposed to a play date, especially since my kids had already met him.

"I'd like that. Where you want to take them?"

"Maybe Dave and Buster's or another arcade. It'll

have to be on a Sunday because my next few Saturday's are crazy."

The waitress came over to check on us before bringing the check, and I couldn't believe how well the date had gone. I almost didn't want to leave Houston's presence. A mature, polite, respectful, fine ass man was a breath of fresh air. After Houston paid, he walked me to my car, and my breathing hitched as he invaded my personal space.

"Drive safe," that deep timbre wafted into my ears and made Miss Kitty thump. His body was lightly touching mine. He wasn't doing too much. Shit, I almost felt like he wasn't doing enough.

I cleared my throat and shifted my weight from one leg to the other nervously. "I will. Thank you for dinner."

When Houston used the pad of his thumb to stroke my cheek while he peered into my eyes, my stomach caved in. Why was this man so alluring? "Have a good relaxing night." He licked his lips, and I almost had an orgasm right then and there. I wanted to relax on his dick, but I kept it cute.

"I'll do that."

Houston stepped back, and when I unlocked the door, he opened the door for me. I picked the boys up, and we cuddled on the couch and watched a movie. I had texted Houston and let him know I made it home, and that turned into us texting each other for the remainder of the night. I was going to try my hardest to take Kimbella's advice and keep my heart out of it, but that would be hard as hell to do. I hadn't even gotten the D yet, and Houston had me smiling and blushing like I didn't have good sense.

Chapter Eight

HOUSTON

It was Monday morning, and I pulled up to my shop ready to get to work for the day. The first thing I noticed was a guy standing outside the door smoking a cigarette. The shop was open because my receptionist and my other tattoo artists were inside, so I wasn't sure if buddy had an appointment and he was just outside smoking or what. But if he didn't have an appointment, he had to get from in front of my shop. I got out of the car, and his gaze landed on my face.

"Yo, Houston. My name is Jordan, and I'm Mike's cousin on his mom's side. I just wanted to link with you and see if we could start seeing the girls. They don't come around my family like that, and it's fucked up."

I looked him up and down and drew back a bit. "Mike's cousin on his mama side? Nigga, I don't know

Mike's mama, and I don't know you. Y'all had seven and eight years to form a bond with those girls. I don't know what to tell you because I don't know you, and they can't go anywhere with you."

Jordan flicked his cigarette on the ground. "Dig this, I'm trying to be respectful, but this shit is pissing me off. You're not their daddy, nigga. You don't even take them to see Mike. Just because yo' dead ass sist—"

I hit that nigga so hard, he flew back into the door of my shop. I didn't even give him a chance to recover before I was on his ass throwing punches like a mad man. Rage had my blood boiling, and my nostrils flared like an angry bull as I beat the fuck out that nigga. My receptionist, Jazzy, ran out of the shop and attempted to pull me off the nigga, but she had no luck. I'm not a lil' nigga, and I'm in the gym heavy. Her petite ass couldn't do nothing with me while I was angry and damn near trying to kill this idiot. It took me hearing my homie Ransom's voice for me to stop pummeling Jordan's face and take a step back. I glared at him as my chest heaved up and down, and his mangled face was already swollen and bruised. I didn't know how he was going to drive home because his eyes had already started to swell shut.

A retired rapper by the name of Ransom was my first appointment of the day, and he ushered me into the shop because people were starting to crowd around and look. I didn't want the police at my place of business, but this man had me fucked up if he thought he was going to pull up and disrespect my sister. Remembering his words had me ready to turn around and go right back outside to handle his goofy ass.

"Yo, you good, homie?"

I had done nine of Ransom's tattoos in the past. At this point, there was hardly any free space left on his arms or his chest, so he'd moved over to getting them on his back. The largest tattoo I had ever done on him took me two and half hours to do, and over the course of the years that I'd been tattooing him, we'd become friends. Ransom was a cool guy, and he had his head on straight. Even before he retired, he didn't live like the average rapper, always wilding out and doing every drug under the sun. He had homes in Winter Crest, Miami, LA, and Diamond Cove.

"Hell nah. That nigga come talking about he's related to the girls on their father's mother's side, and he wants them to start coming around. I don't know that nut ass nigga, and he came out his mouth foul about my sister. After that, it was a wrap for his ass." I went over to my mini fridge and pulled out a bottle of liquor. It's very rare that I tattoo under the influence.

I generally don't drink or smoke before I tattoo anyone, but I needed a shot or three to calm down.

One of the main reasons that I hated getting angry was because it took too damn long for me to get myself back right. If I let it, this shit would have me in a foul mood for the rest of the day. Not a lot of people knew exactly what happened to my sister, but Ransom did because, as I said, I considered him a friend.

"Had I been here and heard that shit, that nigga would look way worse than he does. Disrespectful ass nigga. I'm sorry you had to go through that, homie, but don't let that nigga take you there."

I thought back to the speech I gave Omi about having tough skin when someone spoke ill about her mother. An angry chuckle escaped my lips because of the irony. I knew kids didn't have good sense like that, but this grown ass man thought he was going to stand in my face and disrespect my sister. If the police came, I'd gladly take that ride to the station and smile in my mugshot. That nigga would never be around the girls. As the tequila I drank burned my chest, a thought entered my mind.

Even though he had a few more years, Mike would be coming home one day. And whether I liked it or not, he was the girls' father, and he had legal rights to them. His name was on their birth certificate. By the time he did come home, the girls would be teenagers, and they could voice where they wanted to live. I knew they loved me, but that nigga was their father. Was I prepared for the day that he might come take them from me?

My sister didn't leave anything in writing. I took the kids because it made sense with the way my parents worked. I had to go through a process to become their legal guardian, but that was easy because she was deceased, Mike was in prison, and I was the girls' uncle. I never even thought about the fact that he might come home and be able to take them from me. That shit had a nigga's chest tight.

If Mike had ever shown me that he was a decent father, I'd have no objection to him coming home and getting his daughters, but he was a terrible boyfriend to my sister and a shitty father to the girls. He was always broke, and he took my sister through the most. When he came home from prison, it would take him some time to get on his feet. I didn't want the girls leaving a comfortable, stable home to go follow him to the unknown, but I didn't have legal rights over them.

One shot wasn't doing it, so I had to toss back another. Ransom is my homie, but I still didn't want to be unprofessional, so with a slight scowl still on my face, I started getting my station ready to do his tattoo.

"How is Indiana and the baby doing?" I asked him trying to get my mind off the bullshit that had just occurred.

"They're good, man. London sleeps all day and is up all night, but you know I'm a night owl anyway. After Indiana goes to bed for the night, I'll get up with London for her next two feedings, which are usually around midnight and four in the morning. When she wakes up around seven, Indiana gets up with her, and I sleep for a bit. During the day, we both take care of the baby and do light housework, but we have a cleaning lady and a chef. And my mom comes over every other day and tries to take over. The other day, I had a business meeting, so she went over and let Indiana get a nap in. Shorty slept for three hours. Some days, London kicks our ass," he chuckled.

"I'm sure; that newborn phase ain't no joke."

"Hell nah, it isn't, but I wouldn't trade it for the world. Indiana isn't a leasing agent anymore, so she only does real estate. She had a closing two days before she went into labor, and she's just been home chilling for the past two months. She plans to go back to work when London is four months old, but you know as a real estate agent, she can do a lot of her work from home. When she has to meet with clients or show homes, me or my mom can watch the baby. She probably won't go back to selling houses full time until the baby is around a year old, but by that time, I'm gon' be trying to put another one in her."

I laughed. "Oh, y'all want 'em back to back?"

"She said she wanted to wait at least two years, but I'd have them back to back if it was up to me. This is the part of life that I was ready for. I'm not technically retired because I have artists that I manage, but I also have a team working for me, and I can move how I want to move. I don't have any issues with sitting in the house with my kids while my wife works. I'm already rich. I want to lay back, chill, and enjoy life. I want three or four kids, but Indiana told me I was smoking dick. She almost got popped in the mouth saying that dumb shit. When you gon' start? I mean, I know you have your nieces, but you gon' put one in Tiesha any time soon?"

I chuckled. "Hell nah. We broke up. She's not ready for kids, and that included my nieces. Before my nieces came, I wasn't in a rush to have my own. I just felt like it would happen around the time that I was thirty. But I'm single now, and I damn sure don't want to have kids with just anybody, so I'll be chilling for a minute."

"Nothing wrong with that. You know me and Amaya weren't on the same page, and that's ultimately why she left my dumb ass at the altar. Even though I knew she wasn't the one for me, I didn't want to be the one to back out, so thank God she left me hanging. She did me a huge favor, and after she did that, it took me no time to meet someone that

I'm on the same page with. Sometimes, we have to go through bullshit to get to the good shit."

"I feel you."

Conversing with Ransom calmed me down. I'd never been into the streets, but I had homies like Zeke that were about that life. I didn't judge, and I'm cool with everybody, from drug dealers to athletes and rappers. I have friends that want to sex a different female every night, that make broads take plan B's, pay for abortions, and have no plans of slowing down any time soon. Then, I know men like Ransom that cherish their women. They treat them like royalty, they provide, and they live for the families that they created. They aren't in the club every weekend, and their fun consists of traveling and having cookouts versus throwing kickbacks and hanging in the hood all day.

Men like Ransom reminded me of my father, and those were the guys that I went to for advice. I gravitated more towards them because even though I didn't have biological kids, my nieces sat me down, and gave me a new outlook on life. I had already been practicing for the past year, so if a woman came along, and I saw that she was the type I could build a family with, then so be it. But I wasn't pressed in the least.

* * *

Later that evening, I sat my nieces down and had a talk with them. I had worked late, so we didn't get to eat dinner together, but we had cheesecake together before their bedtime. "Do you guys want to start visiting your father more?" I asked.

Terrionna's eyes lit up, but the ever-passive Omi just shrugged. "Yes. I like seeing my daddy," Terrionna replied.

"What about you, Omi?" I asked as my gaze landed on her face.

"I guess. He used to be mean to mommy sometimes, and then after they would fight, he wouldn't come see us for a long time."

Terrionna gave her sister an exasperated glance. "That was a long time ago, Omi."

"Not really," she mumbled.

"Listen. You two are your own people. You don't have to do what you don't want to do, and you don't have to do what the other does. If one of you wants to visit him and the other one doesn't, that's fine too. He is your father, true, but I'm not going to make you go visit him." I could damn near see the relief oozing off of Omi.

I instructed the girls to go brush their teeth, so they could go to bed, and they hugged me and took off for the stairs. I had almost asked them if they would want to live with their father once he came home, but the conversation was already a little heavy, so I just left well enough alone.

I would never say anything to try and make the girls look at their father sideways, but just from the way Omi responded to my question, I doubted I'd have to worry about her going to her father when he came home. Terrionna might be a different story, but that was still a few years away, so I refused to keep dwelling on it. I grabbed my blunt from the coffee table and went outside on the porch to smoke. As I exhaled weed smoke from my lungs, something told me to call Cypher.

"Hey," she answered, and I could hear the faint sound of music in the background.

"You just getting off?"

"Yeah," she sighed. "I worked both jobs today, and mama is tired. I'm going to get the boys now. How was your day?"

"My day was eventful. It sounds like you could use a good massage."

She groaned. "Don't even mention that word around me. I have so much tension in my body that if anyone, male or female, rubbed this shit out of me, I just might fall in love," she giggled.

I had the girls, and she had her sons, so it wasn't like we could just link when we wanted to, and that's why some of my homies didn't like to date women with kids. "The next time you have some free time and can get away, I'll definitely do that for you. If you fall in love, that's on you."

"I'll keep that in mind."

"You about to get the boys, go home, and get ready for bed?"

Cypher sighed. "Yes. So I can get ready to do it all over again tomorrow. I'll talk to the boys about their day on the way home, go over homework, then get them in the bed, eat, take a shower, and get in my own damn bed, hopefully in enough time that I can at least get six hours of sleep before I have to be up again. I'm about to be working like crazy because the boys' birthday is in five weeks, and that's an expense that I have to prepare for."

"Their father doesn't help out at all?"

Cypher kissed her teeth. "The last thing he bought them was a pair of Jordan's almost two years ago. That sorry ass nigga does nothing for my kids. He doesn't even acknowledge their birthday. I bet if someone put a gun to his head and asked him when his kids' birthday was, he wouldn't know the answer."

I could hear the disgust in her tone, and I knew it was written on my face. Niggas like him were the worst kind, and I had no respect for them at all. "Lame ass nigga" I seethed. "Well, you sound like you need a vacation and a break. You want to go to Florida with me and the girls next month? Your kids could celebrate their birthday a little early. I'll pay for the plane tickets and the hotel room."

I was met with silence, and I was prepared for Cypher to try and reject my offer. "Houston, that's too much."

"Why is it too much?" I pulled from the blunt.

"Because we just met. We went out on one date, and you're talking about three plane tickets and three tickets to Universal Studios? I know that will cost a lot, and I'm just... I don't know..."

"You think if I spend that kind of money, I'm going to feel like you owe me something?"

Cypher laughed. "I'm not even going to say what I want to say."

"We're grown. Say it." The weed made me loose and relaxed. The night air felt good as hell, and my body was finally at ease after the day I had.

"I was going to say I'd have sex with you right now, so I wouldn't care if you did feel like I owed you something."

I wasn't expecting that, and it made me laugh. "Damn, it's like that? So what's the issue?"

"Honestly, I don't even really know what the issue is. I can be a very prideful person. I don't like asking people for anything, so the few times I asked Nick to buy his sons diapers or help me with expenses, and he refused, it made me angry, and made me feel stupid. I've just become accustomed to doing things on my own, and if my own child's father won't give me $100 a month, it's just hard to believe that a stranger will spend thousands without batting an eyelash. I'm just not used to that."

"I'm a very humble person, so I never want you to feel like I'm bragging, but I'm blessed. I tatted my homie today and while most people's friends want discounts, the nigga paid full price and hit me with $100 tip. I don't even expect tips, but every time I tatt a celebrity or someone with money, they tip me anywhere from $100 to $500. I've had a job in the past that I hated, but I had to get up every day and go because I had goals. Seeing you raise your kids alone and work as hard as you do, tugs at a nigga's heartstrings. If I can afford to help you, and I'm offering, then let me. Being stubborn just gon' have yo' ass overworked, underpaid, and angry all the time. If I can't help to make your life easier, I don't need to be in it."

"Damn. That's the realest thing a man has ever said to me. I've for sure been out here dating some men with little boy mindsets. You're really a breath of fresh air, and I know we're supposed to be keeping it light because you're newly single, but you are really showing me that I was giving the time of day to some lame ass men."

"When you know better, you do better, babe."

"I just arrived at my parents' house, and these

little boys are about to talk my head off, so I will text you before I go to bed, okay?"

"You do that."

She did me a huge favor, and after she did that, it took me no time to meet someone that I'm on the same page with. Sometimes, we have to go through bullshit to get to the good shit."

Ransom's words sounded off in my mind. I had no clue what would become of this situation with Cypher, but she had her head on straight for sure. If she could be patient with a nigga and give me time to be single for a minute before jumping into something else, she just might prove to be the one for a nigga.

Chapter Nine

CYPHER

"Please don't look at my feet," I said to Houston after he picked my legs up and placed them in his lap. "I need a pedicure ASAP. I just haven't had time to get one."

My feet aren't ugly, but the gel polish on my toes had grown out, and my nails were a little too long for my liking. I hadn't had a pedicure in almost a month. Even though Houston offered to pay for me and the boys to go to Florida, I had still been working like crazy because I wanted to buy some new clothes for the trip and have my own spending money. I knew what he said about me not being stubborn and letting him help, but it was just in me to try and do things on my own. The one time I got comfortable and tried to let Nick play the head of the relationship and pay the bills, it left me damn near homeless when I had to scrape and spend everything I had every month to pay rent that he stopped paying. I didn't want an eviction on my credit for seven years, so I was pregnant working like a dog to make sure that rent was paid every month, and that shit left a bad taste in my mouth. It was hard to depend on a man after that because I knew if he didn't do what he was supposed to, I would be the one to suffer in the end not him.

See, Nick didn't have good credit when we moved in together, so my name was the only one on the lease. When he stopped paying the rent, it didn't affect him in any kind of way. Had we been evicted, my credit would have been just as shitty as his. Lesson learned the hard way. It was my first day off from both jobs in over a week, and the boys were in bed. I had the next day off as well. I was taking five days off to go to Florida, which would still leave me with four days' worth of PTO, and I was using one because I was dog ass tired. After I took the boys to school the next day, I planned to come home and sleep for a good three or four hours. That's how tired my body was. I was looking forward to Florida so bad. Something had to give because I couldn't work like this for the rest of my life.

Houston did exactly what I told him not to do and started inspecting my feet. "They pretty though. And soft," he pointed out.

We had taken the kids to Dave and Busters, and they had a great time. Houston had the cutest nieces, and Terrionna complimented me every five minutes. Omi was a lil' quiet, but they were both polite and well behaved.

"Thank you." My teeth sank into my bottom lip as he began to rub my feet. I couldn't remember the last time I had my feet rubbed, and Houston was working magic.

He rubbed my feet with the right amount of pressure and aggression, and I could just imagine what his hands would feel like massaging the rest of my body. As if he could read my mind, Houston looked over at me.

"You down for that massage we talked about a while back?"

All I could do was nod. He had no idea how much I was looking forward to it. At my full-time job, I sat down all day, but that didn't prepare my body for all the standing and walking I did at my waitressing job. I barely even got the chance to take a fifteen minute break, so after leaving one eight hour job that was mentally draining, I went straight to a four or five hour shift and was on go pretty much the entire time. At thirty-three, I wasn't exactly a spring chicken, but I was too young for my back and legs to ache the way that they did.

I was dressed in short, black night shorts and a gray sports bra, so I didn't have many clothes on anyway. There was a candle burning in my room, but

I cut the television on, so Houston could have a bit more light. I lay on my bed on my stomach, and he started with my shoulders. I stifled a moan as his hands massaged my shoulders then moved down my back. My eyes fluttered closed, and I let out a content sigh as Houston did his thing.

By the time he moved down to my thighs, my vagina was pulsating. Houston's massage was half putting me to sleep and half turning me on. I had only had one professional massage in my life, and he had the woman that did it beat by a long shot. I almost didn't want him to stop. Until I felt him plant a soft kiss on the nape of my neck, and my yoni started contracting something serious.

I bit my bottom lip as Houston began to French kiss my neck while his hand massaged my ass. He moved his hand around and eased it into the front of my shorts. His mouth moved over to my ear, and he strummed my clit with one finger while he sucked on my earlobe, making me moan softly. I already knew that sex with Houston was going to be an experience that I might not be prepared for. Sex with Nick was cool because I loved him, but in my entire adult life, I'd never had sex that was so mind-blowing that it literally had me hooked on the D.

Houston didn't half step with anything that he did, so I was willing to bet money that he wasn't slacking in the love-making department. Houston removed my shorts and gently bit my ass cheek.

"Stay just like that. Don't move," he instructed and got off the bed.

He stood up and removed his clothes. I heard him tearing a condom wrapper open, and he placed it on his manhood before getting back on the bed and kissing me from the crack of my ass, up my spine, and back to my neck. He spread my ass cheeks apart, and I moaned as he entered me. His dick was huge, and he pushed into me a few inches at a time until he was completely inside of me.

Houston stroked my walls slowly, allowing me to get a feel of his girth and length. He put me in a headlock from behind and increased the pace of his strokes as my eyes rolled into the back of my head. "That feel good?" he spoke into my ear, and the bass of his voice sent a chill down my spine.

I nodded as Houston kissed the corner of my mouth. I turned my head to the side and snaked my tongue into his mouth. We kissed passionately as his strokes intensified, and before I knew it, I was moaning into his mouth as my vagina muscles contracted on his dick, and I came.

Houston eased out of me and turned me over onto my back. He slid back into me, and I whimpered as I locked my legs around his waist. I wasn't trying to fall in love with this man, but I was so wet, and he felt so good. I made the mistake of lifting my eyes, and I caught him staring down into my face. Our orbs locked, and I remained stuck on stupid peering into this man's eyes while his dick made me feel things I didn't need to be feeling.

"Fuck this pussy good," he grunted before crushing his lips into mine, and we engaged in another passionate kiss.

I cradled the back of his head with one hand while he buried his face in the crook of my neck. His grunts and soft moans made my clit swell. When Houston swirled his tongue around one of my nipples then took as much of my breast into his mouth as he could, I came again, and my mind was blown. I had never even given myself back-to-back orgasms. No man had ever, and I knew then that Houston was dangerous as hell.

Houston pulled back and peered into my eyes. "You 'bout to make a nigga cum, baby."

The way he said *baby*, made my pussy tighten on his manhood, and my eyes fluttered closed as he moaned one last time and released into the condom. I would just lay there and let this nigga tell me anything. A story from his past. A lie. I didn't give a damn. His voice was so soothing to me, yet erotic at the same time. Houston could be speaking about the weather, and it would make my clit swell. I hated when he pulled out of me because that meant the moment was over, and though he was far from a minute man. I wanted more. I was addicted already from one sex session. God help me.

I was glad I had a bathroom in my bedroom, so he wouldn't have to go clean up in the bathroom that the boys used. One of them found their way out of their bedroom at least once every night to either use the bathroom, get something to drink, or ask me some random question. I bit my bottom lip nervously as I put my clothes back on and prayed I could get Houston out of there without him running into the boys. I wasn't yet ready for them to know that I had company in my bedroom.

Single parents are restricted in a lot of ways. It's hard for us to even get our rocks off when we have kids while the absentee parent can be out there moving carefree and with no fucks to give as if he or she doesn't even have kids. I wouldn't even be able to sleep at night if I had kids in the world that I didn't do for, but everyone doesn't think the same.

I leaned against my dresser and waited for Houston to emerge from the bathroom. When he did, I couldn't stop the smile that spread across my face. This man was too fine, and as I suspected, he didn't disappoint in the bedroom at all. If I could go to sleep to that dick every night, I'd probably start walking bowlegged. I took in his long, thick wicks and thought about how God showed out when he made the black man.

Houston walked up on me and pressed his body into mine. "What you smiling at?" he stared down at me as he gripped my waist, making my body temperature rise.

"No reason. Let me walk you to the door before one of these nosey ass kids wakes up and catches me."

Houston eyed me for a few more moments, then he stepped back, and I tried to steady my breathing as I walked him out of my bedroom and to the front door. "Text me and let me know you made it home safely."

"Will do." Houston reached in his pocket, pulled some money out, and placed it in the waistband of my shorts. "Pedicure on me tomorrow." He winked at me and walked out of the door before I could object.

After I closed the door, I removed the money and counted it. I shook my head at the three hundred dollars. That was one expensive ass pedicure. I don't get long, over-dramatic, nails with a bunch of designs, so my fills are never more than $40. I could get a pedicure, a fill in, my brows waxed, and still have money left over. That damn Houston was going to mess around and have me wanting to turn his ass every which way but loose. The female that let him walk out of her life just because she couldn't accept his nieces was crazy as hell. Shit, just call me step mommy dearest.

* * *

"Please don't get on this plane showing your ass. Please don't go on this trip showing your ass. Houston was nice enough to invite us on this trip with him and his nieces, and if you embarrass me, we will never go anywhere else. Got it?" I gave the boys a pep talk as we walked outside to the Uber that was going to take us to the airport since I didn't feel like driving or paying high ass parking fees to leave my car at the airport.

The boys simply nodded. They were so excited to be getting on a plane for the first time, and all I could do was thank God that Houston made it happen for them. He was a wonderful man, indeed. Before he invited us to Florida, I had already worked some overtime and started using my tips from the job to pay down my credit card balance. I was determined to give the boys a great birthday, but I wouldn't have been able to top Florida.

With the extra money that I had saved, I was able to get them all the things they wanted for their birthday, and since the trip was a week before their actual birthday, all the gifts were hidden at home. The little things that Houston had done for me thus far, like paying for my oil change, giving me money for my pedicure, taking the boys on a trip, it showed me just how much easier my life would be if I had a man that was about something in it. Just as he'd said, a significant other was supposed to make your life easier, but I had never experienced that. Life was so stressful and chaotic with Nick that you couldn't convince me relationships weren't some bullshit. But now I understood the difference between being in a relationship with a boy versus a man.

The boys talked a mile a minute on the way to the airport, and I alternated between texting Kimbella and scrolling social media. At my big age, I'd never flown before. I didn't take any trips before I had kids, and once I had the boys, I couldn't afford to take myself anywhere. I was lowkey a bit nervous myself, but it just wasn't about flying. I was nervous just from knowing that I was about to be around Houston for the next few days. I had done something I don't normally do and taken myself shopping in preparation for this trip because I wasn't about to be around his fine ass looking dusty.

I had ordered some cute pieces from Fashion Nova and Shein, and I got my hair braided. I even splurged and got some contacts and my lashes done, so I could give my glasses a break. For the airport, I was dressed comfortable but cute in a black, long-sleeved dress that hugged my body and went all the way down to my ankles. It was a Skims dupe that I found on Shein because why pay over $50 for a dress when I could find one that looked just like it for $15?

The closer we got to our boarding gate, the more nervous I became. I know I'm not an ugly woman, but something just had me feeling like a man like Houston was out of my league. He must like something about me though, right? Shaking off all doubt and negative thinking, I concentrated on having an amazing vacation with my boys. One that we all deserved. As we neared the gate, Houston came into view, and I bit back a smile. He had his head down looking at his phone, and he was dressed in black sweats and a black hoodie. His nieces sat beside him with their iPads in hand, and they were all engrossed in whatever was on their screens.

We had another ten minutes before our flight boarded, and there were a few empty seats directly across from Houston, so me and the boys made our way over. Houston must have sensed my presence because he looked up and smiled at me and the boys.

"What's going on?" he extended his fist to bump with the boys.

"Thank you for taking us on this trip," Quentin remembered what I had told him to do. "We've never flown before."

"Yeah, thank you," Qori chimed in.

"How could I not invite the two best football players in Diamond Cove?"

That made the boys smile wider than I'd ever seen them smile. "You good?" Houston asked. "You look nice. First time I've seen you without the glasses." I observed the lustful gleam in his eyes, so I knew he must have liked what he saw.

"Thank you, and yes, I'm good. I'm right there with the boys in the sense that I've never flown before. I'm trying not to be nervous," I admitted as my stomach felt like it did a back flip.

"You've never flown before? Damn, why not?"

I shrugged. "Never got around to it before I had the boys, and after them, vacations weren't really a luxury I could splurge on. Even when I used to get my taxes every year, I'd have to pay my rent up for a few months to put myself ahead, get new furniture, a new car, and anything else I couldn't afford throughout the year. Vacations were just never a priority. Well, let me clarify that. I've taken trips before. They just weren't out of the country or super far places, and I always drove rather than flew."

Houston nodded his understanding. "Gotcha. Well, we about to change all that." He winked at me, and my stomach did another backflip.

This man had the ability to make me lose all of my common sense, and I didn't like that thought. I was enjoying him though. We weren't in first class, but Houston had paid for priority boarding, so we were able to get on right after first class boarded. We found our seats and prepared for the hour and a half flight to Florida. Once the plane ascended, I was in a trance looking at the world below me. I had always known that I never wanted to work just to pay bills, but being up in the air solidified it. I wanted to travel, have fun, and create dope ass memories. Working every day *just* to barely have enough money to live was no longer cutting it for me. I couldn't afford to let one of my jobs go to go back to school, but something had to give.

Once we landed in Florida, I was on cloud nine. We took an Uber from the airport to the Airbnb, and when the kids saw the house, they went crazy. The house had four bedrooms, and two of the rooms had double beds, so the girls could share a room, the boys could share a room, and me and Houston had our own rooms. There were also three bathrooms in the house, a pool table, and a huge pool in the backyard. The shiny white tile floors were so clean you could eat off of them. The house was immaculate.

Universal Studios wasn't until the next day, so Houston had arranged for a chef to come over and cook for us. He left to go to the grocery store, and I stayed there with the kids while he shopped for snacks and breakfast food. He even came back with a bottle of tequila for us. While the chef cooked, I sipped my tequila and chilled in the pool with the kids who were all having the time of their lives. I was in heaven. Damn. Imagine living like this on a regular basis.

By the time the food was done, the kids had been in the pool for over an hour, and it was getting dark out. Houston took over, while I simply chilled and drank my liquor. When dinner was done, he instructed the kids to take showers and get ready for bed because we had a long day ahead. After the boys were tucked in, I took a shower myself, and by the time I was done, my ass was drunk. Drunk and horny. I entered the living room and found Houston on the couch looking at television. He had already showered as well.

"You not going to bed?" I stood in front of him.

Houston's gaze lifted, and he licked his lips. "You gon' put me to bed?"

"You already know." I smiled devilishly.

"Say less."

Houston stood up, and I followed him to his bedroom.

Chapter Ten

HOUSTON

The trip to Florida was like that, and now it was back to the real world. We'd actually been back for three days, and I was pulling thirteen- and fourteen-hour days at the shop. When I have a lot of days blacked out where people can't make appointments, it's always crazy after that. I was right back to being booked up for the next few months, but I didn't mind. I don't mind working on Sundays, but on this particular one, I wasn't working until late because I was bringing Terrionna to visit her father.

We went through the process of getting into the visitation room. Omi chose not to come, and I wasn't going to make her. We waited for about five minutes before Mike came out, and as soon as Terrionna's gaze landed on him, her eyes lit up. I wasn't against her loving her father at all. I just hoped he'd never end up disappointing and hurting his girls the way he did my sister. Don't get me wrong. I know plenty of niggas that aren't shit, and they take their women through it. I don't blame Mike for my sister committing suicide. At some point, everyone will get their heart broken. It's life. If he lied, cheated, played games, or whatever, I wished my sister had been resilient enough not to let it break her. I could get past him being an ain't shit boyfriend but an ain't shit parent wasn't acceptable ever.

He lifted Terrionna off the ground, and she wrapped her arms around his neck. "Where's your sister?"

"She didn't want to come."

"Oh yeah? Why not?" he looked from Terrionna to me. "Omi okay?"

"She's good. She just didn't want to come."

Mike sat Terrionna down and sat down. "You're the adult though. You gave her a choice on coming to see me?"

"You're damn right I gave her a choice because I'm not making her come anywhere she doesn't want to come. If she wanted to see you, she'd be here."

I could tell Mike was pissed, but I didn't give a damn. He knew better than to keep talking to me, so he directed his attention towards Terrionna. For an hour, she told him about school, Florida, what she wanted for Christmas, and all that. When I was ready to have a conversation with Mike that she didn't need to hear, I gave her some money and told her to get some snacks from the vending machine.

"I'm not sure if you've talked to your cousin Jordan or not, but I suggest you teach your people about boundaries. I don't need anybody I don't know approaching me about the girls because them being related to you will never be enough for me to just let my guard down and give them access to the girls. And the next time that pussy comes out of his mouth sideways about my sister, he's going to get way more than his ass whooped," I gritted in a low tone.

Mike sighed and sat back in his seat. "If Jordan disrespected your sister, then he got what he got. But I'm the girl's father. It's only fair for them to know my side of the family too."

"Nigga, fuck yo' side of the family if it ain't your daddy. How many times did you pick those girls up and take them around yo' people before you got locked up? You were never a full-time father. Not even when you lived with my sister. She worked and paid the bills, and you used to bitch about babysitting your own kids. You better be lucky I even bring them to see you because there were times when you were free that you'd go months without going to see them. You never been 'bout shit, but I'd never tell my nieces that. The older they get, they'll see that shit for themselves. That's why Omi not fucking with you right now. She already remembers."

Mike's nostrils flared, and I knew he was pissed, but I didn't care. I glanced over at Terrionna and decided to get one more thing off my chest before she came back.

"The girls live in a nice house in a nice neighborhood, and they go to a good school. I have Omi in therapy, and the girls are learning to adjust to life without their mother. You might be their father, and once you're released, there might be some things that I can't keep you from doing. But if you ever think you're going to take them from me just to have them living crazy and mistreating them, you got me fucked up."

"I appreciate everything you've done for my girls, but I'm not understanding the point of you talking to me crazy today."

"'Cus, nigga, you not shit, and I watched you fuck my sister up. I'll never let you do that to my nieces."

Mike wasn't able to respond because Terrionna ran back over to the table, and we deaded the conversation. But I meant everything that I said. Mike could play with me if he wanted to.

* * *

"What are you doing for your birthday?" Vannah asked me hours later as I did a tattoo on her thigh. I had fucked around with Vannah a few times before I met Tiesha. I cut her off when I got serious with Tiesha, and she ended up with a guy named Kedrick. Vannah and I have the same birthday.

"I hadn't even really thought about it. I just got back from a vacation with the girls, and my books are pretty full. I did take the day before and the day of my birthday off, but I don't have any big plans. What you got going on?" I wiped excess ink from her tattoo.

"I was going to Rolling Loud in Miami with this hoe ass nigga, but we broke up. I paid for the tickets, and he never even reimbursed me, so if you want to go, you can. I'm staying in Miami for three days, but you can be in and out. Just go to the concert and give me some birthday dick. I won't be mad at that," she giggled, causing me to laugh.

I'm not a social media nigga, so I'd never tell my business on any of those apps, but I did delete the pictures of Tiesha off my page. She'd made a few posts about being single, but I didn't even read all of them. I wasn't sure if they were thirst traps because she wanted niggas to hit her up, if she wanted me to see them or what, but I scrolled right on by like I didn't see them. I'm sure she didn't know that all she was doing was sending women to my DM's. The same females that liked her pictures and commented on her shit, came straight to a nigga's messages to see what was up with me, and I had ignored every last one of them.

Cypher was cool as hell, but I wasn't trying to be serious with any female at the moment. We had some good ass sex in Florida though. We went through six condoms, and the last night when I didn't have another one, I bit the bullet and hit her raw. That pussy was like that, and the best part of the trip was watching her interact with the girls. I had explained to them that Cypher was just my friend, and as far as the kids knew, we slept in separate beds in Florida. I didn't want to bring another woman around them too soon, but her interaction with the girls was genuine, and I liked that shit.

She had them in the kitchen with her. She let them help her cook, and she was always so patient with them. She was fair about everything and never favored her sons over them. They all got the same exact treatment, and I knew it was real when Omi laid her head on Cypher's lap when we were all gathered in the living room watching a movie. She'd never been anything even remotely close to affectionate with Tiesha.

That made me like Cypher that much more, but I wasn't trying to rush things. I really had to get back into grind mode, but work wasn't the only reason I planned to fall back from Cypher for a few days. I just didn't want to do too much too fast and have her getting attached to me, and I didn't want the girls getting attached to her.

I thought about the dates for Rolling Loud and gave a slight nod. "I can do that. I'll fly out for like a day and a half. The girls can stay with their grandfather. He's been asking to get them anyway."

"Yayyyy, I'm excited," Vannah squealed.

I knew she wasn't lying when she said she wanted some dick, but Vannah also knew that going to Miami with me meant she wouldn't have to come out of pocket while I was there. I'm not a dope boy, and I'm far from rich, but I'm extremely comfortable. The rent that the other tattoo artists pay me to utilize my shop is enough to cover the mortgage and the bills every month. Everything I make from tattooing is straight profit, and I can make $500 on a light day. People love tattoos, and there are guys that will spend $300 on one tattoo and be back three days later getting another one.

I also have investments. My pops put me on to investing when I was twenty. I've only invested into three separate stocks. One I cashed in on after a year. I invested $800, and I cashed out at $3,056. The second one, I invested $4,200, and four years later, it was at $29,500. The third one, I just invested in two months ago. I invested $8,000, and it was only at $10,100. Soon, I want to get into buying artwork. When the girls turn eighteen and graduate from high school, I want them to have a nice lil' savings set up for them to enter the real world with whether they choose to go to college or go straight into working. Life wasn't just about me anymore. Being that my sister committed suicide, life insurance wouldn't pay out any money, so my dad handled her funeral and everything. There was nothing that we could pass down to the girls.

I also have credit cards with five figure limits that I barely use, so when a nigga wants to do a lil' something, I can definitely afford to do so. A month before me and Tiesha broke up, I'd even started pricing rings in the event that I proposed to her in the near future. The ring that I felt she might like the most was $17,000, and I would have copped that for her with no hesitation. Glad I didn't jump the gun and spend my money.

I finished Vannah's tattoo, and she told me she'd be in touch about the trip to Miami. I was going to be twenty-nine, and while every birthday was special, I just didn't care about going all out this year. My thirtieth was going to be a movie, but for now, I was cool with keeping it light. I had too many goals and too much to do to be extra with the celebrating. I was proud of how far I'd come, but I had a long way to go.

Chapter Eleven

CYPHER

This was the reason Kimbella told me to keep my heart out of shit. It had been two weeks since we got back from Florida, and in that two weeks, I had only talked to Houston four times. I knew that he was busy with the girls and work because I was busy too, but I'm scrolling on Instagram the other day, and I see this nigga at Rolling Loud with some pretty brown-skinned chick that looked like B. Simone. Just the thought of them being in Miami together and him sexing her the way he sexed me made me want to throw up. I couldn't be angry at him because he was a single man doing what single men do. I was mad at myself for being jealous and for caring. It wasn't his fault that it's so hard for a woman to find a decent man to entertain; meanwhile, men can find a pretty female like birds find worms.

I could be dating multiple men, living my best

life, and having great sex, but these men were creeps. Most of the men that reached out to me via social media made me want to throw up in my mouth. Even the ones that looked good and dressed nice because most times, I knew that was all they had. Clothes and social media likes. I literally know a guy that lives with his mother, doesn't have a car, and is a dead-beat dad, but every time he posts a picture on social media decked out in designer clothes, he gets like 200 likes in ten minutes. The thirsty ass comments from women make me chuckle because, baby, if only you knew.

The sounds of the boys arguing wafted into the kitchen, and I groaned. I had been trying to ignore them because I didn't want to be that person that was in my feelings about a man and took it out on my children, but they were doing too damn much, and I was tired. Those little boys literally argued about everything. It was barely eight pm, but I was done with them for the night. I dried my hands and went into their room.

"Cut the game off and get in the bed. You have literally been arguing since dinner two hours ago, and I'm tired of it. Goodnight."

I cut my eyes at them as they groaned and kissed their teeth. Quentin had the nerve to throw his controller, and I was two seconds off his ass. I stood in the doorway and waited until everything was put away, and the television was off.

"Brush your teeth and go to bed," I stated in a calm tone.

The boys marched towards the bathroom with scowls on their faces, and I went to the kitchen to pour myself some wine. My phone rang, and I saw that Houston was calling, but I wasn't going to answer, just like I didn't answer when he called me the day before. By the time I saw his Instagram post, Rolling Loud had already happened and was over. I assumed he was back in Diamond Cove, and I knew if I talked to him, I'd have an attitude and be in my feelings. That would make me feel pathetic because he wasn't my man. So, I was choosing to ignore him until I was in a better mood.

I poured a glass of wine, grabbed a bag of potato chips and my phone, and went into the living room. I had already showered, and I was giving myself an hour to watch TV, drink wine, and relax before I got in bed. I had to work both jobs the next day, and I wasn't looking forward to it. As I watched television, I thought about Houston, and I started feeling guilty for ignoring him. He had taken me and my boys on a vacation that wasn't cheap, and my sons had the time of their lives. He didn't owe me anything. Guilt won, and after taking a big gulp of alcohol, I picked my phone up to call him just as a text message came through.

Houston: Unlock the door.

My brows furrowed, and I hopped up off the couch. Sure enough, when I looked out of the blinds, he was getting out of his car in an empty space right in front of my building. I bit my bottom lip to keep the smile from inching across my face. I watched until he disappeared, and then I waited for the sound of his feet on the stairs. I moved over to the door and looked out of the peephole, and the moment he came into view, I opened the door.

"I was just about to call you. How did you know I was home?"

Houston gave me a look like he felt I was full of shit. "You were just about to call me, huh?"

"I really was. I promise. I just got the boys to bed, and I picked up my phone to call, and your message came through."

"I went by the restaurant, and you weren't there. So I came to make sure you were good, 'cus you have to be fucked up and damn near on your deathbed to be ignoring me."

I chuckled. "Not on my damn deathbed. Like I said, I was about to call you. I'm sorry."

Houston walked up on me and stared down into

my face. "Why you been ignoring me? What I do?"

I didn't want to nag. I didn't want to sound like a brat or turn him off. I could blame it on work and being busy, but I decided to just go ahead and tell the truth. "Okay, I'm not mad. I promise. I just saw you in Miami with another woman, and I felt some kind of way. Not in a way like I didn't want to talk to you again. Just in a way like I needed to step back and take my feelings out of it. That's all."

He nodded. "I can dig it. You're a woman, and y'all are crazy, so I get it."

I grinned and pushed him playfully. "Anyway, nigga." I walked over to the couch and sat down. "So, was Miami fun?"

"Yeah. It was alright. Me and shorty that invited me have the same birthday. She bought tickets for her and her dude, and they broke up, so she gave the ticket to me. I only took the day before my birthday and the day of off, so I flew out and came back the next day."

"Happy belated birthday. Why didn't you say anything? I could have gotten you a card or something."

Houston shrugged. "I make a big deal out of kids' birthdays, but I'm a grown ass man. If I want to take a trip or buy somebody something, I will, but I rarely go all out for my birthday or treat it like a national holiday."

"My birthday is a national holiday," I joked. "I don't care how much overtime I have to work. I always save up to do what I want to do on that day that I can afford. I can't wait 'til the day I can spend birthdays in Dubai or some shit. Until then, tattoos, dinner, and the club works for me."

"How my lil' homies doing?"

I rolled my eyes and drained the wine from my glass. "Your lil' homies came real close to getting their lil' asses whooped tonight. I know siblings bicker. Trust me, I get it. But lately, those boys argue about everything, and it drives me crazy. But the kicker is, they can't stand to be apart. Earlier, I told them tomorrow, one of them can stay with my parents while I work, and the other can stay with Kimbella, and they cried. They hate being apart for more than an hour, but they argue like cats and freakin' dogs."

"Terrionna and Omi are the same way. Me and my sister never argued. From day one, she was always my protector, and I was hers. Most siblings do argue though. My homie Zeke and his brother, Tony, have fought more times than I can count. I mean, will lock up like two grizzly bears and tear some shit up."

"I wish I would see Qori and Quentin fighting like that. I'll mess both of them up. How are the girls? Has Omi been staying out of trouble?"

"Surprisingly, she has. I don't know how long it's going to last, but I have my fingers crossed. I don't want her to go to an alternative school, but if she gets sent there, there isn't anything I can do about it."

"She's the sweetest kid. She's just a little rough around the edges, but she's been through a lot," I sympathized.

Houston looked at me with hooded lids. "I've been through a lot too. Can you make me feel better?" he asked lustfully, and I laughed.

He grabbed my hand and pulled me onto his lap. I straddled him, and he caressed my ass and sucked on my neck. "I missed you," he whispered, and my kitty became instantly moist.

"Is that right?" I asked as I closed my eyes and enjoyed the feel of his tongue on my flesh.

"It is."

I pulled back and peered into his face for a bit. "Let me make sure these bad ass kids are asleep."

I eased off his lap and walked to my kids' room. I peeked in the door, and they appeared to be knocked out. I walked back into the living room and grabbed Houston's hand. I led him to my bedroom, and minutes later, we were undressed in my bed, and he was sucking on my breasts. Houston gave both my breasts adequate amounts of attention, then he placed a trail of kisses down my stomach. When he latched onto the inside of my thigh and began to suck, my back arched slightly. I caressed his head as he passionately kissed and sucked my thighs. When he made his way down to my peach and locked his lips around my nub, I gasped with pleasure.

Houston moaned as he sucked and licked me slowly and sensually. He was eating my vagina like he was making love to it, and I was whimpering and squirming because I couldn't be as vocal as I wanted without waking up my kids. I hadn't been eaten out in a long time, and Houston was performing magic with his mouth. I cupped my breasts in my hands as he ran his tongue down the crack of my ass then went back to sucking on my pearl.

"Houston, baby," I whispered softly as I felt an orgasm brewing in the pit of my belly.

"Let that shit go," he mumbled into my pussy, and I did just that.

My mouth fell open, but no sound came out as my body spasmed, and he sucked and licked up every drop. By the time Houston entered me, there was puddle underneath me, and I knew I was going to have to change my sheets. Houston snaked his tongue into my mouth and kissed me passionately as he stroked me aggressively. He was sexing me with just the right amount of roughness, and I loved it.

I sucked on his bottom lip and moaned as he hit me with long, deep strokes. My essence ran down the crack of my ass as I became wetter and wetter. "You wanna ride this dick?" he asked, and I nodded. I wanted that dick however he gave it to me.

Houston flipped me over, so I was on top of him, and I stared down into his face as I rode him to the best of my ability. I loved it when he moaned. It turned me on even more, and it made me want to give him the ultimate pleasure. I leaned down so we were chest to chest, and I sucked on his earlobe. Houston gripped my hips and slammed me up and down on his manhood. The last time he lifted me up, I felt his warm seed shooting onto my belly and my thighs as he released with a grunt.

Ignoring his sticky essence, I kissed him and eased my tongue into his mouth, and we kissed passionately for almost a minute before I got up and went to clean up. He joined me in the shower, and round two began. By the time Houston left my apartment an hour and a half later, I had three orgasms, and he had two. I forgot all about the fact that he'd been in Miami with another woman, and I went to sleep with a smile on my face.

* * *

The next day, I hadn't heard from Houston all day, and the moment I was crying and in my feelings, he called. I almost didn't answer, but I was on a break, and I decided to go ahead and see what he wanted.

"Hello?" I tried to blink back my tears, but I

didn't do a good job of masking the pain in my voice.

"What's wrong? You good?"

"Not really. I will be though. I'm just being a baby."

"What's wrong, baby?" The soothing tone of his voice instantly made me feel better. It was crazy how just having someone to vent to that actually cared what you were going through could lift your spirits.

"I signed up for overtime at my full-time job because the property taxes are coming up due on my car. They're $145, and I need an inspection and to renew my tags, so all together that will be a little over $200. I always try and get overtime for extra expenses. So, at the last minute, they changed my kids next game from Friday 'til tomorrow when I have to do the overtime. I already asked for Friday off from the waitressing job. Once you sign up for overtime here, you have to work the shift, or you get written up. I'm just tired of missing their games. My friend can't go because she has a doctor's appointment, and my mom has to take my dad to physical therapy."

"If it's at four, I can go. My last tat for the earlier part of the day is at two, and my next tattoo isn't until seven."

My eyes widened. "You'd really go to their game for me, so they don't have to be there with no one in the stands for them?"

"Yeah, why not? I've been to one of their games before, and I took my lil' homies to Florida for their birthday. I honestly enjoy watching all of the kids play, but your sons are nice. I swear by the time they hit high school, nobody will be able to fuck with them on the field. They're going to make it to the NFL and retire you. Watch."

I smiled at the same time that tears filled my eyes. "Thank you so much, Houston. In the short time that I've known you, you've been such a blessing to me and my kids. I feel like I could never repay you. I swear you don't know how good this just made me feel. Sometimes, there are whole families that show up for the kids, and most times, it's just me and my parents or me and Kimbella for my kids. Their father has never seen them play. I just don't want my kids to grow up feeling like they don't have a support system."

"You don't have to explain to me. I get it. I swear I do. And me and my nieces will be there."

Just like that, I was in better spirits, and I talked to Houston for the remainder of my break with a smile on my face. I swear, if I hit the lottery that man can get half. I've never run into anyone like him, and I believed he was absolutely genuine. I didn't even want to consider the fact that he was acting, and he wasn't who he portrayed himself to be because then, I'd be crushed.

Chapter Twelve

HOUSTON

It was a Saturday, and Cypher was off from the restaurant. My cleaning lady was sick, so Cypher agreed to come over and clean for me and cook for all of us since I didn't have to go to the shop until eight pm. One of my earlier clients had to reschedule because she had the flu. I was sitting on the couch with the twins watching a football game, and Omi and Terrionna were in their room watching Frozen for the hundredth time when I heard screaming.

"No! We're not watching it again. Your stupid tail always want to watch stuff back to back. It's my TV too!"

Omi was going in. I stood up and headed for the bedroom when I heard Terrionna chime in. "Uncle Houston said I can watch what I want!"

"How you gonna watch it with no TV?"

Terrionna screamed, and I entered the room just in time to see Omi pushing the television off the dresser. It fell to the floor and broke, and Terrionna started crying.

"Fuck is wrong with you?" I barked so loud that Omi jumped. I have never cursed at her before, but watching her purposely break a television just to spite her sister was surreal to me. I had never seen her display that kind of anger.

I was marching towards Omi, and I must have had a mean ass scowl on my face because she screamed, and Cypher came out of nowhere and jumped in front of me. "I can't tell you how to discipline your nieces, but not while you're mad. Houston, calm down, baby."

Her eyes darted back and forth across my face as my chest heaved up and down. I had just steadied my breathing when Omi screamed. "I hate being alive! I wish I was dead like my mommy!" she ran from the room, and my heart dropped.

I took off after her, but it wasn't so I could punish her. Omi ran into the bathroom, and before she could slam the door and lock it, I pushed my way in. She slid down the wall crying, and I ended up on the floor with her in my lap, hugging her while we cried together.

"Why did my mommy leave me? I miss her. I miss her so bad."

I hugged Omi tighter, and she wrapped her arms around my neck and buried her face in my neck. "I miss her too, shawty. Your mommy was my first best friend. We did everything together." I rocked Omi from side to side. "She was the only person that knew all of my secrets. I miss her every day, and I think about her every day."

Omi lifted her head and removed her arms from around my neck. "I'm sorry I made you cry." She wiped my tears, and I smiled.

"You didn't make me cry. I cry for your mommy all the time. I wish I could have saved her, but baby, you see the way we all hurt, and we all miss your mommy. Don't you ever in your life think you can do what she did. I already lost half my heart when she died. Losing you or your sister will take the rest of my heart. Don't do that to me. Please. We can get through this as a family. I love you, and your sister like you were mine. You can tell me anything, and you can talk to me about anything."

"I'm sorry I broke the TV. Sometimes, I just get so sad then I get so mad. I try to count to ten in my head, but it doesn't always work. I'm going to try harder. I don't want you to be disappointed in me."

"I love you, Omi. Nothing will ever change that. I want you to be better for you. I don't want you to be sad or angry, and anything I can do to help you, just tell me. I'd walk to the end of the world for you with no shoes on if that would make you happy."

She wrapped her arms back around my neck and put her face back in my neck. We stayed in that position, not speaking for about fifteen minutes. "I'm going to apologize to Terrionna now. I'm sorry."

"You're good, baby. Apologizing to your sister is a good idea."

She left the bathroom, and I stood up and leaned against the wall. Just when I thought this shit was getting a little easier, I always got hit with a curve ball. Cypher entered the bathroom, with empathy in her eyes.

"Is she okay?"

"She will be."

"Are you okay?"

I nodded, but Cypher must not have believed me. She walked into my personal space and wrapped her arms around me. She stepped back and smiled at me. "Your nieces are so lucky to have you."

"Are they?" I asked seriously because some days, I didn't know what in the hell I was doing.

"Are you kidding me? Heck yes, they are lucky to have you. I haven't even known you that long, and me and the boys are lucky to know you. You are an awesome guy, Houston."

"Thank you."

"No thanks needed." She kissed me on the lips, and we exited the bathroom.

No one ever told me this road would be easy but got damn.

* * *

Monday afternoon, I left my accountant's office, and a nigga was happy as hell. I'd just cashed out on the second investment that I had ever made, and I had a check for $43,000 in my hand that I was taking straight to the bank. I had come up with the idea to get some vending machines. I was going to start out with two and put them in my tattoo shop. Then, I was going to get two more and put them in my homie's barber shop. Ransom also told me I could put some in his office because his artists always come in there with the munchies and shit. I just wanted to get to the point where I had multiple streams of income, and I never had to worry about money. I did okay for myself, but it was time to do better than okay.

I knew that me, and Cypher banked with the same credit union, and all I needed was her name and her phone number to put money into her account. I then swung by her job at the restaurant and requested to be seated in her section. Since knowing Cypher, I had slept with Vannah twice. Women flirted with me every day, and while I still wasn't ready to be in a relationship, Cypher was probably the one that got the most time and the most dick from me.

"Hi." She smiled when she approached the booth and saw me seated there.

"I just wanted to give you this. I'm going to order some food too, but this is the main reason that I came by." I handed her the deposit slip, and she looked at it confused. "I put $5,000 in your bank account. Five bands won't make you rich, but it should help you out, so you can chill on all the overtime for a minute."

I wasn't surprised when tears filled Cypher's eyes. "Oh my God, Houston. Thank you." Tears spilled over her eyelids, and that shit warmed my heart.

Cypher was one of the rare women that I met that didn't feel like because she was fine or for giving a nigga the pussy, I owed her something. If a man is having sex with a woman, I see no issue with him helping her out, but too many women feel like they deserve the world from a man out the gate just because he's interested. Cypher is a woman that works hard for her and her kids, and she fucks with me because she wants to. Not so every time we have sex, I can buy her a bag or an expensive wig. She works like crazy with a purpose. For her bills, for her kids. Rarely for her own personal reasons, and I knew if her kids' father helped her out, she'd be able to work less and spend more time with them.

Her gaze landed on my face, and she stared at me for a second, probably trying to figure me out. She snapped out of her trance for a few seconds before shaking her head. "I know what you're going to say, but still, I don't know how I could ever repay your kindness."

"Make sure when my order comes, it's piping hot and good as fuck." I winked at her, and she smiled.

"I got you, and I'll bring you food for the girls that you don't have to pay for and don't even try," she added sternly. "What do you think they'd like?"

I ordered for the girls, and Cypher scurried off to put my order in. It was nice seeing her so appreciative. Maybe if there were more random acts of kindness in the world, it would make people have a little more faith that things could get easier for them, and they wouldn't be so quick to give up. My phone alerted me that I had a text message, and I saw that Vannah was hitting me up for some of a nigga's time. I was horny, and I knew that by me giving Cypher five bands, she'd probably be more than willing to sex me like a porn star. I didn't want to crack on her for some pussy after giving her money because I didn't want her to feel as if I felt she owed me anything, so I texted Vannah back and told her to meet me later tonight at the shop.

Chapter Thirteen

CYPHER

I was walking on cloud nine in the mall with my boys the day after Houston gave me the $5,000. I damn sure wasn't going to blow the money on shopping, but I felt I deserved at least a new coat and a few outfits. The check I had coming in had overtime on it, and I had made pretty good tips the night before, so I was confident that my financial situation was about to be good. I was tempted to quit my job at the restaurant, but I couldn't jump the gun like that for $5,000. Maybe once I got my income taxes and paid some things like my car insurance up for the year, I could think about quitting. For now, I was just happy that I wouldn't have to work anymore overtime for a month or two at least.

I had never in my life met a man like Houston, and the fact that he was younger than me blew my mind. I know there are providers out there, but I had never run into one. He wasn't even my man, and he had done more for me than anyone of my ex's ever had.

"You guys want something from the food court because I'm not cooking tonight," I said to the twins after I had purchased coats for all three of us. The weather would be changing soon, and I wanted to go ahead and get that out of the way. The boys had hit a little growth spurt, so a lot of their winter clothes were going to have to be replaced.

"I want Hibachi," Quentin wasted no time answering while Qori pondered the question.

"Is that..."

Before Qori could even get it out of his mouth, I looked up and locked eyes with the devil himself. Or better yet, Nick. And the kicker was, he was walking alongside a pregnant female, and they both had bags in their hands. That got a laugh out of me, and he looked like he wanted to crawl under a rock.

"Hi, dad." Qori waved loudly, and I had to cover my mouth to keep from doing the most. Nick was far from being the boys' favorite person because he was a lying ass waste of space, but I knew Qori only did that to be petty. He was indeed my child.

The woman that Nick was with snapped her head in his direction and stared at him with a slack jaw. Maybe she didn't know he had kids. Nick approached us sheepishly and pulled some money from his pockets. Like the pathetic nigga that he was he handed the boys $25 each. I never talked bad about him to or around the kids, but that was the last damn straw. My upper lip curled, and I gave that nigga the most hateful glare that my face could form.

"Nigga, you in here with bags from Foot Locker, Foot Action, and Dr. Jay's, and you give my kids that you haven't done anything for in years $25?" I drew back. "You are the sorriest nigga on the face of this fucking earth. I tried to be the bigger person and not put you on child support, but I will be down there first thing Monday morning because this shit is ridiculous. You really walking around like you got it like that while you have two kids that you ignore and neglect. I hope you rot in hell!" I stormed off with the boys hot on my heels. I was pissed.

The world was really full of men like Nick, and it was sad as hell. If he had another child on the way when he had no relationship with and didn't take care of the two he already had, that was even more pathetic. I thought I stopped letting Nick upset me a long time ago, but the way my heart was racing, and the scowl on my face told another story. The only thing that made me feel slightly better was that Qori and Quentin appeared truly unbothered.

It was sad when children had to grow thick skin in order to not be hurt or disappointed by the actions of their parents. It made me feel like shit for even procreating with a man like Nick, but there wasn't anything I could do about it now. I got our food to go, and we headed for the car. They talked a mile a minute in the backseat, and by the time we reached our apartment, I was calm. While we all sat around the kitchen table eating, I fought the urge to call Houston. I was too grown to be at the point where I was somewhat playing games, but I didn't want to do too much. No matter how much Houston had done for me, the fact remained that he was newly single and not trying to jump into another relationship. I didn't want to become clingy and give him the impression that I wanted more than he did.

As I was cleaning the kitchen, I decided to stop being stubborn and call him. He answered fairly quickly, and the music and chatter in the background let me know that he was at work. "Hey. I was just calling to check in and see how you're doing."

"I'm good, lil' mama. How are you?"

The smile that stretched across my face was ridiculous. I hated the effect that Houston had on me. "It was good. I took the boys to the mall, and we got new coats. They haven't argued once since they've been home from school, so I have to say it's a pretty good day."

Houston chuckled. "I'd say that was a good day

indeed. Hold on for a second. Where you getting this at, Love? Oh, okay."

"You have some tape or something where you can cover up my nipples? I mean, I don't mind my breasts being out, but you might have a girl or something, and I don't want to cross any lines."

My face scrunched up at the voice of the thirsty female that Houston was about to tattoo. I rolled my eyes inwardly chastising myself because I should gone with my gut and not called the nigga. Houston could be single all he wanted to be, but that didn't mean I wanted to hear him flirting or see videos of him out of town with other women.

"I'm single, baby. I have some tape, but I'm with whatever you with."

I rolled my eyes again, and that time, I rolled them so hard it's a wonder they didn't get stuck. Ole girl giggled, and Houston came back to our conversation.

"What you about to get into?" he asked in that sexy baritone that I now knew wasn't only reserved for me.

"Just about to take a shower and watch some TV. I'll let you get back to work."

"Aight, babe. Talk to you later."

I wasn't even comforted by the fact that he called me babe. Shit, he'd just called her ass Love. I knew I was tripping and doing too much, but I was going to allow myself to be in my feelings for a few moments before I put my big girl panties on and shook it off. I wanted to be one of those women that claimed a man could do what he wanted to do as long as he paid like he weighed when it came to me, but Houston was so damn fine, I didn't *just* want his money. I was being greedy as hell, and I wanted the entire package. His time, his affection, his dick, *and* the money. I couldn't name one bad thing about him. He was lovingly raising his sister's kids, and he was a guardian angel when it came to me and my situation. His personal hygiene was immaculate, and he had the art of making love down to a science. This man was an alien.

Just take it for what it is and enjoy the ride. Don't ruin things by being overly dramatic.

Those were the kinds of pep talks that I had to give myself to keep from moping around and being in my feelings like a dummy.

* * *

A few days later, I was sitting in Kimbella's backyard as her and her husband threw one of their infamous Spades game. Aside from Kimbella, her sister, and her next door neighbor, I was female number four among six men. We were taking turns playing, and the ones that weren't playing were eating, drinking, and mingling. The kids were in the house playing the PlayStation on the huge television that was mounted on the wall in the den.

I had met Kimbella's cousin once before, and though he was cute, he rubbed me the wrong way by flirting with me while he had a wedding band on his finger. That had been a little more than a year ago, and according to Kimbella, he was now divorced. I didn't ask her specifics, but divorced is what he needed to be if he made flirting a habit. I didn't want to deal with a man that I knew had a history of cheating, but at the same time, dating didn't always have to equate to a love connection. Houston had shown me that conversation and occasional dates with men was better than not interacting with them at all. I damn sure didn't have to marry Ronnie or even be serious with him to let him compliment and attempt to impress me. I knew as soon as he started trying to have sex, I was out. This kitty was reserved for Houston, but I'd converse and go out on dates with other men.

"When you gon' stop playing and let me take you out?" Ronnie asked as I sipped my drink.

I still had to drive myself and the boys home, so I was trying to pace myself. I eyed Ronnie over the rim of the cup. "Didn't you *just* get divorced? You not trying to take any time to heal?" I asked sarcastically.

Ronnie kissed his teeth. "Hell nah. I was married

for four years, and I was miserable for three of those muhfuckas. I want to live life and have fun. That's where I'm at in life right now. I want to have fun. Three weeks out of the month, I work six days a week. The one week of the month where I have three days off, I like to be out of the house doing something. One thing I'm going to do is eat good, drink good, and listen to some good music. I like car shows, comedy shows, trivia nights at bars, wine tastings, you name it."

Men killed me. They would hound a woman to take her out on a date. Take her on one date where they barely spent $100 and spend the next few months trying to sit up in her house, eat the food she cooked, and lay up in her bed. Ronnie might have been different, but only time would tell. My phone vibrated, and it took everything in me not to smile as I read over his text message. I focused my attention back on Ronnie.

"I work two jobs, and I have twins, so time isn't something I have a lot of, but you can call me."

He grinned as he pulled his phone out, and I called my number out to him. Kimbella's husband called Ronnie over, and I took the opportunity to text Houston. I wasn't drunk, but I was tipsy enough where the mere thought of his dick had me horny as hell all of a sudden. I knew Kimbella's party would be going on for another two hours at least, so I got the idea to sneak off and get a quickie in with Houston. A devilish smirk crossed my face as I typed swiftly. I wasn't sure if he was at work, but I'd find out soon enough.

I damn near squealed with excitement when he replied back to my nasty message and told me he could be at my apartment in twenty minutes. I made my way over to Kimbella and put her up on game. She looked at me with a wide smile on her face.

"You know the boys are good while you go get that back blown out."

"Thank you, friend." I wasted no time grabbing my keys and making a quick but discreet exit. If the boys came looking for me and saw I was gone, they'd blow my phone up. The objective was to get in and out before I was missed.

As soon as I got home, I ran to the shower because I'd been sitting outside for three hours, and I wanted to smell like soap and lotion for Houston and not outside. I had just tied the belt on my robe when he rang the doorbell. Houston was taking a break from work, so he didn't have time to waste, and that was okay with me. The moment he crossed the threshold of my apartment and shut the door behind him, he tongued me down passionately and used his body to walk mine to the bedroom.

He removed his clothes and was sucking on my breast when my phone rang. I only grabbed it off the nightstand to make sure it wasn't my kids, and when I saw an unsaved number, I placed it back down on the nightstand. Houston's lips found mine, and we kissed as he pushed into me. I locked my legs around his waist as he rocked in and out of me. I'd had some amazing sober sexin my life, but drunk sex would always take the cake. And drunk sex with Houston was enough to make me profess my love for him while my eyes rolled in the back of my head.

It didn't take me long at all to cum long and hard, and I was in an extra freaky mood. "Let me taste it," I whispered in Houston's ear.

He pulled out of me, and I got on my knees and took him into my mouth hungrily. My head bobbed up and down as I sucked like my life depended on it while his deep grunts and masculine moans turned me on even more. I hated that we had to engage in a quickie and that I couldn't take my time with that D.

Houston released into my mouth with a loud grunt, and my phone started going off again. Ignoring it, I sucked up every drop before going to the bathroom to brush my teeth, rinse my mouth out, and clean up.

"What in the hell?" I snapped as I walked out of the bathroom, and my phone was going off again with the same unsaved number. If that was Ronnie, he was going to get blocked because there was absolutely no reason he should have been calling me that much.

"Damn, that nigga thirsty, huh?" Houston asked with a smirk. "Answer and tell him you with daddy."

I kissed my teeth. "You should know all about thirsty people. You have enough of them in your tattoo chair, your IG comments, your birthday trips," I sassed, making him laugh.

"That's cute. I like it when women act jealous. It makes me feel special."

I rolled my eyes. "Using the word jealous would be reaching," I lied.

"If you want me all to yourself, you can just say that," he stated while walking up on me and pressing his body into mine. I swallowed hard and made the effort to keep my cool.

"Boy, please. Date and have fun. Enjoy being single because I'm doing the same."

"Is that right?"

"Yeap."

"You must have put it on that nigga 'cus he blowing you the hell up. I should've brought my gun in with me."

"Don't get ahead of yourself. I haven't put it on anybody. I haven't had sex with anyone other than you in months. It's not going down like that over here. Dating doesn't mean sex."

"I'm just fucking with you. That's nice to hear though. I like exclusive pussy."

"While you give out community dick?"

Houston laughed. "Now you're the one getting ahead of yourself. I wouldn't call it community dick. I'm not out here giving it up like that."

"Ummhmmm," I stated as I got dressed.

"I'm about to head back to the shop. Later." Houston smacked me on the ass and kissed me on the lips simultaneously.

When the unsaved number called me again, I answered the phone with an attitude because whoever it was blowing me up like that better have a damn good reason. "Yes!" I snapped into the phone.

"Whoa, why you got an attitude? I was just calling to make sure you were good because you left the party quick."

"I had to make a quick run, and Kimbella knew I was leaving. That's all that matters. I didn't have to check with anyone else. You've called me like four times. That's a bit much."

"Well, excuse me for being concerned. I just wanted to see if you were already in for the night. I wanted to talk to you some more."

"Yeah, that's not going to work out. Me and my ex just got back together," I lied and ended the call.

Trying to date after a man like Houston was going to be hard as hell.

Chapter Fourteen

HOUSTON

I stood by my car with a stoic expression on my face as Tiesha pulled up in my driveway and parked behind my car. I waited impatiently for her to get out of her car and tell me what she wanted. She walked over to me with a pained expression on her face.

"That's where we are now? You won't even answer the phone for me?"

"I was busy when you called me, Tiesha. What's up? I have to pick Omi up from the shop. I'm having a birthday party for her today, and I'm really in a rush."

Tiesha let out an exasperated sigh. "I know you hate me. I know you do, and that kills me because I still love you, but I'm in a bind. I loaned my mother $1,800 to bond my brother out of jail, and she only paid me back $800 making me $400 short on my rent. I know you're not obligated to help me, but I can't get evicted. If I can just ge—"

"I'll send the money to your Cash App. Is that it?"

Tiesha breathed a sigh of relief. "Thank you so much, Houston. I swear you just saved my life. You know you can still hit me up to braid the girl's hair. I don't mind doing that for you."

"I'm good. I have someone that will braid their hair, but thanks for offering."

Tiesha nodded and walked back towards her car. I might look like a sucka for sending her $400, but that was going to be the last thing she ever got from me. Everyone loved having access to a good guy until him being a good guy inconvenienced them. Me raising my nieces wasn't the life that Tiesha wanted to live, but she played on the fact that she knew I wasn't a spiteful person, and I wouldn't want to see her homeless. That was my last act of mercy for her though. I didn't have anything else for her. I had just spent over $1,000 for Omi's tenth birthday at an indoor gym that had ziplining, trampolines, and other activities for kids. The party, plus her gifts, and cake had cost me a little bit, but it was a special occasion. She invited a few of her cousins, three of her friends from school, and I invited Cypher's kids.

When Cypher arrived at the venue, she texted me and asked me if I could come to the front. I gave the boys dap and showed them where to put the gift and where to go. "What's up?" I noticed that Cypher looked pale, and she had a blank expression on her face. She was dressed in gray sweats and a white tee with flip flops on her feet.

"I wouldn't normally drop the boys off and not stay with them, but they really wanted to come, and I don't feel good. I want to go back home and get in bed for just an hour. I'll be back to get them as soon as the party is over."

"You're good. You don't have to stress that. You okay?"

"Yeah. I think it's a little bug or something coming on. Working two jobs and running to games, being a mother, and just not resting enough period I think is catching up with me. I might have lost my waitressing job because I called out, but I don't even care. There are a million restaurants in this city. I can find another job."

I gave a slight nod. "Don't worry about the boys. They're good with me. The girls' grandfather wants to take them for the night after the party, so I can bring them home. You don't have to come back and get them."

"Thank you so much. I really appreciate that."

I could tell Cypher didn't feel good because it didn't even look like she'd brushed her hair. It was pulled back in a bun, but sprigs of hair were loose. If she wanted some time to herself to catch up on some rest, I didn't mind looking after the boys. I never had an issue with them. The party went off without a hitch. Omi was on her best behavior, and I was looking forward to a night out with my niggas.

When I took the boys home, I went inside the apartment, and Cypher was curled up on the couch eating soup. I sat down while the boys told her about the party before taking off for their rooms. "You sure you good?" I looked over at her, and Cypher's gaze remained on the television.

She refused to look at me, and my brow hiked up. I didn't speak, but I was staring at her wondering why she was ignoring me. After a few moments of awkward silence, Cypher pulled an object from behind the pillow on her couch and extended it towards me. Before it was even in my hand, I knew what it was, but I took it anyway. The word, ***pregnant***, jumped out at me. Cypher's gaze was back on the television screen.

"We fucked up," she stated solemnly. "I know better, and I still played with fire. I'm just not used to dealing with someone on a regular basis, and I got carried away. I guess my dumb ass felt that since it's been nine years, I wouldn't get pregnant that easily. I didn't even really think about it. Plan B's or nothing crossed my mind. Just fucking stupid," she shook her head. "I've never had an abortion, but there's a first time for everything."

"That's what you want?"

Her eyes darted in my direction. "What do you mean is that what I want? I'm already a single mother of two kids. I know you would take care of your child. I know that without a doubt, but the fact remains that I have to carry this child while working two jobs. Then what about the six weeks I have to take off for maternity leave? I struggle enough with two kids. Three will be a lot. I'll have to move to a bigger apartment which means more rent. I know you'd take care of the baby, but I still have to take care of myself and the boys, and three kids will just make that harder on me."

"I can't make you do anything you don't want to do, but if you think you'd have to work two jobs while carrying my baby, you don't know me at all. I'd never even let you do that shit."

"I'm not trying to be difficult, Houston. I swear. I like you, and I like getting to know you, but you said yourself you weren't trying to rush into anything seri ous. Even if we're not a couple, co-parenting is serious. You have the girls. I have my sons. It just seems li—"

"It seems like you have a lot of excuses, shawty. I like the fact that you're weighing all the pros and cons, but there are worse things we can be than two mature adults that co-parent. You being pregnant doesn't have to stop us from getting to know one another. We have nine months."

"I absolutely love how you make it sound so easy. Just give me a day or two to think about it. Okay?"

"I can give you that. I'm about to head home and take a shower. You sure you don't need anything?"

"Nope. I'm good. I have soup and Ginger ale. The boys do have a heart because when they know I don't feel good, they're usually on their best behavior."

"I like the sound of that. They weren't any trouble at the party either. I think they get along well."

"Yeah, they do," she smiled at me. "I hope Omi likes her gift. I'm not used to shopping for girls."

"She loved it. Even though she acts like a brat sometimes, she's not hard to please. She told the boys thank you."

"Sounds good to me."

I gave her a slight nod and left the apartment. In my car, I blew out a deep breath. That was the last thing I was expecting, but I knew how babies were made, and we had slipped up a few times. I for sure should have been more careful, but I was caught up in the heat of the moment. After being with Tiesha for so long, I hated condoms. And she was on birth control, so I got into the habit of not pulling out. Cypher's shit was so snug and wet that I got caught slipping. A child was something I wanted eventually, so it's not like the news was the most devastating thing I ever heard, and there were worse women I could have gotten pregnant. I was going to let Cypher make the ultimate decision since it was her body, but I would probably be lowkey pissed if she got rid of my seed.

I went home and got ready to meet Zeke and Ransom at the strip club. As soon as I walked in the section, I peeped that Zeke looked stressed. He was holding a bottle of Azul by the neck, and though he wasn't a light weight, I knew he couldn't drink an entire bottle of liquor by himself, but if he was drinking straight from the bottle, he could have that shit.

"You aight, homie?" I asked Zeke as I gave Ransom dap. There were a few more bottles in the section and a variety of chasers. With all the liquor we had, it was way too much for the three of us, but what we didn't finish, we would usually give the females in the club. They loved being gifted expensive ass bottles by strange, handsome niggas. I've had hella pussy thrown at me just off the strength of giving females half-empty bottles of liquor.

"Hell nah, I'm not okay. I messed up bad." Zeke shook his head and took a swig.

I could take a guess on what messed up bad entailed. "You got caught cheating again?"

"Hell nah, but the shorty I did fuck with is pregnant. Man Cresha is gon' kick my ass."

My brows lifted. There wasn't even anything I could say because he had indeed messed up bad. "Go ahead and let me know what you want to be buried in." I was dead ass serious too.

Ransom shook his head. He hadn't known Zeke for as long as I had, but they were cool enough for him to have met Cresha a few times. As far as I knew, Ransom was faithful to Indiana, and I had never cheated on Tiesha. I didn't want to judge Zeke, but his ass just had to go and play with fire, so it was hard to feel sorry for him.

"Play stupid games, win stupid prizes, nigga. I heard last time she left you, you were sick. What's the logic in doing it again?" Ransom asked Zeke.

"Man, nigga, I don't know. Fucking temptation. I love my girl, but there are some fine ass thick ass females out here, and they be throwing it at a nigga. I've turned down all advances for three years, then I slipped up with a fucking IG model," Zeke groaned, throwing a full on tantrum.

"This broad has a baby by a rapper. She drives a G wagon and lives in a half a million dollar house. Do you know how it stroked my ego that she wanted to fuck with me?"

"Why in the hell does she want to have your baby?" Ransom asked seriously, but I laughed.

Zeke kissed his teeth, and Ransom held his hands up in surrender.

"I'm just saying. If she's a legit IG influencer with a lot of followers, then she gets paid to post and probably has some paid sponsorships, but I can guarantee that house and the car came from the rapper. Broads like that usually don't have kids by niggas that aren't in the same league or higher as their first baby daddy. If this nigga was copping her Birkins and shit, you think she's going to be happy with you getting her Gucci?"

"That's why my ego was stroked, nigga. I hadn't bought her anything, and she took me to her crib and fucked and sucked me like a porn star. Shorty popped a molly and went crazy. She sexed me so good, I dumbed out and paid her portion of the Airbnb and bought her plane ticket to Miami for a girls' trip."

Me and Ransom groaned.

"Niggas, that's nothing," Zeke pleaded his case. "I spent like $500 total. I don't have rapper money, but I'm far from broke. I counted $8,200 last night before I went in the crib. I'm not buying Birkins and shit, but I don't live like a slouch, and she sees that. Real shit though, even I'm confused as to why she wants the baby. Females like her have abortions for fun. I just knew she was going to ask for some money to get rid of this one, but she wants to keep it."

Zeke looked stressed out for real, but again, I didn't feel sorry for him. "If she does decide to keep the baby, you better let Cresha hear it from you and not social media."

"Cresha follows the broad on IG too. She's always talking about how sick the girl's body is."

Ransom and I groaned in unison. "You don't like living for real." Ransom shook his head. "Boy, she gon' fuck you all the way up."

Zeke really looked like he was about to cry, and it took everything in me not to laugh. "Must be something in the water because I slipped up and got somebody pregnant. She already has twins, and she doesn't really want the baby. I told her we can do whatever she wants."

"You're grown and single. This goofy nigga right here has a girl that he's been with for a long ass time. The situations are not the same."

Zeke stuck his middle finger up at Ransom, and I chuckled. "Yeah, but we aren't in a relationship. I didn't wait damn near thirty years for kids to have to do the baby mama thing. I just hope that if she does have the baby, she doesn't switch up on me, and that we can remain cool."

"That one is always a gamble, nigga, but stranger things have happened."

I gave a slight nod before pouring myself a drink. Only time would tell. I got good and drunk and almost ended the night with Vannah. I was just about to text her and tell her I was coming over when I decided to text Cypher instead and see if she was awake. Twenty minutes later, I was rocking in and out of her while our tongues swirled.

"This pregnant pussy good as fuck," I marveled as I spoke into her lips. It seemed as if she'd gotten tighter, if that was possible, and she was definitely wetter and more sensitive. She came four times. I knew my drunk dick was like that, but I think it was the pregnancy.

She had to end up putting a pillow over her face so she wouldn't be too loud. "This shit too fucking good," I groaned as her pussy muscles contracted on my dick, and I shot my seed all into her womb. "Fuck," I panted.

If pregnant pussy was like that, I was about to be in trouble.

Chapter Fifteen

CYPHER

I sat biting nervously on my bottom lip as I waited at my doctor's office. I looked up and saw Houston walking through the door, and it calmed my nerves a little. Three days after I found out I was pregnant, I still wasn't one hundred percent sure about keeping the baby, but I had decided to come to the doctor anyway. Houston was already being super supportive, and I loved that for me. I still wasn't all the way sold, however.

"What's up?" he asked as she sat down beside me, and I peeped the white lady sitting across from me eyeing him. I wanted to say, *fine right*? But I just smirked and ignored her.

"Hey. Just waiting. I've only been here about five minutes."

"Traffic was crazy."

"You're fine."

"Were you able to eat today?"

"Not really," I sighed. One thing I didn't miss about being pregnant was the morning sickness. All I could keep down earlier was watermelon. I tried to eat a bacon and egg sandwich, and I threw it right back up. I tried sucking on sour candy, and drinking ginger. None of it had helped so far. I already hated my job. Having to wake up in the morning and go there feeling terrible didn't help.

I quit my waitressing job because I was still too sick to stand on my feet and wait tables, and I knew if I kept calling out, I'd get fired anyway. I had to focus on one issue at a time, so I was going to deal with later, later. The nurse came to the door and called me to the back. I got up nervously with Houston on my heels. The nurse weighed me, took my vitals, and gave me a cup to urinate in. She also drew my blood and took me in a room to answer some questions. When she was done, she left the room, and I began to get undressed.

"You want me to step out?" Houston asked, and I chuckled.

"Step out for what? You seeing me naked is why we're here."

He grinned and began looking through pamphlets. I hoped he didn't think I was a creep, but I just couldn't stop staring at him. He was even reading the posters on the wall. I could tell if I went through with this pregnancy, that Houston would be involved every step of the way, and that's all I could ask for. Still, the thought of me with three kids was overwhelming as hell. At least the boys were independent in a lot of ways, but I was still nervous.

The doctor finally came in, and she asked me a few questions about my last pregnancy. Whether I carried to full-term, if I had any complications, etc. I took a deep breath as I laid back for the ultrasound because I knew if I saw my baby on that screen, no matter how tiny it was, I more than likely wouldn't get an abortion. I waited patiently for the doctor to say something, and she did after a few moments of silence.

"It looks like your eggs love to come out in pairs."

"Excuse me?" I lifted my head so fast I got a cramp in my neck. I couldn't really tell what I was looking at, but the doctor pointed at the screen for me.

"Sack A and sack B. You are carrying fraternal twins."

My heart pounded in my chest. "Please tell me you're joking."

"Not at all. I'm sure it's quite a shock, but you are having twins. Again."

I erupted into tears, and Houston gave the doctor a helpless look.

"It's a very common response," she assured him.

She talked to me about the prescriptions she was going to write me, told me how far along I was, and my due date, all while tears rolled down my cheeks. When she left the room, I licked salty tears from my lip and sat up. Houston was staring at me helplessly. I'm sure he didn't know what to say. I made no move to get up and get dressed, so he finally walked over to me and wrapped his arms around me.

"It's going to be okay. I promise."

All I could do was cry into his chest.

* * *

Two days later, I sat in one of Diamond Cove's most popular restaurants across from Ransom and his fiancé Indiana. I loved Ransom's music when he was a rapper. Shit, I still listen to his old music like it dropped yesterday. Houston inviting me out with him, and Ransom was the only thing that lifted my spirits after learning that I was once again carrying twins. I wasn't sure what kind of vendetta God had against me. I for damn sure wasn't looking forward to carrying multiples again, but I damn sure couldn't abort two babies. That just seemed cruel. I was miserable when I was pregnant with Qori and Quentin. I started showing at three months, and from the fourth month on, they were so heavy to carry around. Near the end, I'd be in tears some days and still had to get up and go to work. Being pregnant with twins was hard, but being pregnant with twins by a deadbeat was extra messed up.

I knew I wouldn't be able to eat a lot, so I was just ordering light foods like soup and salad. Ransom and Houston were engrossed in a deep conversation, and Indiana started talking about wanting to open a real estate firm in Diamond Cove and needing someone to run it for her, since they spent most of their time in Winter Crest.

"Have you ever thought about real estate?" she asked me as I speared a piece of lettuce with my fork and placed it in my mouth.

"No. I've always heard that it was a hard class to pass, and that the test is even harder."

"It's definitely a challenge. I will never lie to anyone like it's not. And real estate isn't for everyone, but it's not about what you know. It's about who you know, and having Ransom on my team helped me a lot. Most people have to work their way up, but I started selling luxury real estate right away. He was actually my first client. I've only sold one house since I had my baby, and the commission off that was $423,000."

I almost choked on my lettuce as my eyes bulged out of my head. Indiana nodded knowingly. "Wow."

I eyed her diamond-encrusted Rolex, the three Vancleef bracelets on her wrist, the huge rock on her ring finger, and the platinum ring on her pointer finger, while her $6,000 Chanel purse rested on the seat next to her, and I assumed that Ransom spoiled the hell out of her. And maybe he did, but sis had made it abundantly clear that she had her own bag, and I was loving it.

"If you're interested in taking the class, and you can pass the test, I'd love to have you in my office in Diamond Cove. As the BIC, I'd have to get a small percentage of every sale you made, but it would be worth it if you can snag some clients that are in the market for some nicely priced homes."

"I won't even lie to you. I work at a call center, and I hate my job. I wake up every day wondering if this is all there will be to my life. I don't have a degree, and I never thought I'd be able to get a job where I could make a boat load of money with no real skills or education."

"Like I said, I won't pretend that it's easy. But with me putting a few leads in your lap and you taking it from there it can be some great money, and you won't even have to sell a house every month if your commissions are large enough. Say you only made around $10,000 every other month. That's still more than you would make working at the call center."

"You're right, and with me being pregnant, it will be nice to have a flexible job once the babies are here.

Daycare for two newborns won't be anywhere near cheap. If I can make most of my money from home, I'd love that."

"If you're serious, I'll give you my number. I can give you my book, and you can use my study guides. Anything I can do to help you, I will, and the day you pass that test, I'll guarantee I can have a lead for you within a few days. Yes, I want to open an office here, and I need someone to run it, but I also love seeing black women win. I got my start because Ransom looked out for me, and I want to do the same for someone else."

I knew it was pregnancy hormones that had tears in my eyes. I was so grateful. When I found out I was pregnant, I wasn't happy, and when I found out I was having twins, I was devastated. But this had made my night and improved my mood significantly. I wasn't even going to be delusional and think that right away, I could make a commission anywhere near $400,000, but being able to make good money while not dealing with my manager, co-workers, or customers from the call center would be okay with me. It would be more than okay with me. I didn't give a damn if I only made $3,500 a month.

Indiana and I were exchanging information when a pretty female stopped at our table. Well, there were three pretty females, and one of them had on a birthday sash, so it's obvious she was having a birthday dinner. Only one of the pretty women was glaring at Houston like she wanted to kill him. Her friends looked enthralled to be face to face with Ransom. Their disrespectful asses were ogling him like they didn't even see Indiana sitting there.

"This what we doing, Houston? For a man that was so in love with me and never cheated on me, you damn sure are out on a double date real fast. You used to take me on double dates with Zeke and Cresha. Guess you have a routine, huh?"

"One thing I normally refuse to do is explain myself, but I'll make an exception 'cus you got me fucked up. We broke up. That's all that needs to be understood. I wouldn't give a fuck if I was out on a double date an hour later."

Shorty cut her eyes at me, and I raised one brow because I wasn't showing yet. I would be damned if I let myself be disrespected by her bitter ass. If she knew what was good for her, she'd keep it moving because I wasn't above punching her ass.

"Have fun with this low budget ass bitch," she seethed, making me cackle.

I wasn't even embarrassed that she was standing there in Yves Saint Laurent heels, and I had on $98 heels from Macy's. I didn't care that she had on Fendi, and I had on a $25 dress from Fashion Nova. Her calling me low budget didn't hurt me. I was a grown ass woman, and my bills were paid, and my boys were good. I slept good at night knowing that we had a roof over our heads and food in our bellies. That trying to be the baddest bitch shit was for little ass girls with no responsibilities.

"I'd be salty too, if I let a good one like Houston go, but you might want to watch it, sis. I didn't disrespect you, so don't come for me. You don't know shit about me."

Houston took over. "I'm not even the fuck nigga that tells people's business, but you're calling her low budget when you just came to me crying for help on the rent, so you wouldn't get evicted. Fuck away from my table, Tiesha. This is me being nice. You already know how the not so nice Houston gets down."

Tiesha stormed away from the table, fuming, and Indiana shook her head. "If I don't know nothing else, I know females are bold as hell about a man. My baby calmed me all the way down because I stayed ready to tag a hoe's head about that one."

We laughed, and dinner resumed. Later that night, Houston came up behind me while I was in my bathroom wiping off my makeup. "I appreciate you not letting Tiesha get you all worked up. She's not even worth your blood pressure shooting up." He kissed the back of my shoulder and lifted my dress as I eyed him through the mirror.

"I've been looking for one since we met, and I

finally found your flaw. Before me, you had shitty taste in women."

"I won't dispute that." Houston lowered himself, and I was confused until he pulled my panties to the side and ran his tongue down my center. My lips parted, and my mouth hung open, as I threw my head back.

He was going to work on my peach as he gripped my ass cheeks. His nails dug into my flesh, and I bit my bottom lip as he slurped on my pussy like it was ice cream melting on a hot day. When he spread my cheeks and latched onto my nub, my knees buckled.

"Fuck, baby." I whispered as I pinched my extra sensitive nipples.

Essence ran down my thighs as Houston sucked me into an orgasm. I gripped the edge of the sink as my legs trembled. Houston stood up, lifted me up, and sat me on the sink. He peered into my eyes as he undid his jeans, and I matched his stare down. I had the pleasure of knowing this sexy ass man intimately and carrying his kids. I suddenly felt like the lucky one. I hadn't even known I was pregnant for two whole weeks, and he'd already been everything to me that Nick wasn't. I wasn't even panicking about quitting my waitressing job because if he said he had me, I knew he had me.

I moaned and cupped his face in my hands as he slid into me. Houston picked me up while he was still inside of me and placed my back against the wall. "You know you my baby, right?" he spoke against my lips. I hadn't really known that, but it was nice to hear.

"Am I?" I peered at him through heavily hooded lids.

"You are. And I want you and everything that comes with you."

I knew he was talking about my kids, but before I could respond, he snaked his tongue into my mouth. Houston kissed me like we'd been lovers for years, and he was deeply in love with me, and that was enough to make orgasm number two rip through me like a tornado. If I thought about the fact that we would have six kids total, I'd have a panic attack. But something about Houston and his ability to make me believe that he was a man of his word had me oddly comforted.

I held onto his neck for dear life as he sexed me savagely. All I could do was moan his name over and over as he stroked me into orgasm after orgasm, and when my body went limp, he laid me on the bed and ate me out until I had one more.

Chapter Sixteen

HOUSTON

One year later...

I released a deep sigh as I looked at the bucket that was placed in the corner of my tattoo room. It was damn near full from water dripping from the ceiling. I looked up at the brown water stain, and I knew that I wouldn't be able to put off getting the roof fixed any longer. I was far from broke, but that didn't mean I wanted to spend five figures fixing a damn roof. Just six months ago, I dipped into my stash heavy and dropped $25,000 on a six bedroom house with seven bathrooms and a four-car garage. My mortgage payments weren't no hoe, but we desperately needed the space. Quentin and Qori shared a room, and so did Omi and Terrionna. The twins, Rihanna and Rasheed also shared a nursery. Cypher and I told the kids that when Omi turned thirteen, she could have her own room. That would leave Terrionna with her own room too. Then, the boys could separate too.

Rihanna and Rasheed were four months old, and our house was as live as a house could get. The boys still played football, Omi was a cheerleader, and Terrionna did dance. Cypher had gotten her real estate license, and she did most of her work from the office she had in our home. I had to get a huge ass house to accommodate all of us, but it was worth it. Tattooing was going great, and I now had a total of twelve vending machines. The money that I collected every month from the vending machines was enough to pay the car notes on Cypher's new Audi truck and on my BMW truck. I was about to look into getting a carwash.

With all the kids I had, I needed all of the passive income I could get. Indiana stuck to her word, and when Cypher passed her real estate exam, Indiana had a lead for her in two days. It took the woman she was working with over a month to find a house that she wanted, and that her offer was accepted on. She worked the hell out of Cypher's nerves, but she walked away with an $18,000 commission. That was enough to motivate the hell out of her, and she'd been in full throttle ever since. She started off hot, but after the first two months, she didn't sell another house for four months, but that was cool because she had money put up, seeing as how I pay all the bills.

I left the tattoo shop at eleven pm, and since it was a Friday, the kids were up, and I walked into chaos.

"Why you crying?" I heard Quentin say to Qori. "You acting like a punk."

"Shut up!" Qori glared, looking at his brother like he wanted to kill him.

"What's going on in here?" I asked as Cypher came down the stairs looking exasperated.

"That's it. Go to bed. I'm over it!"

"Wait," I said to her and looked at Qori. "Why you crying?" I went over and sat down beside him on the couch.

"Because there's a father/son ball at our school, and our dad won't answer the phone. We won't be able to go."

Cypher kissed her teeth and stormed off, and I glanced at her fat ass as she walked to the kitchen. The twins had put 50 pounds on her total, and after they were born, she only lost 20 pounds of it. When I say shorty had ass for days, that's what I meant. People didn't believe her when she told them she didn't have work done to her body. When she disappeared, I focused my attention back on Qori.

"Why wouldn't you be able to go? Am I not here? I can't go with you? It has to be your real dad?"

I watched Qori intensely while he came up with an answer. Finally, he wiped his tears away and mumbled. "I didn't think you'd want to go with me because you're not my real dad."

My brows furrowed, and I looked at him, truly baffled. "Qori, I live in the house with you, my G. I go to all your football games, and I take you to practice sometimes. I'm at your birthday parties, and I help you with your homework. I might not be your biological father, but I'm here when you need me, just like I am for Omi and Terrionna. I'm not their dad either. Titles don't matter in this house. You tell me when the ball is, and I'm there dressed to impress, making all the other dads look dumb."

Qori nodded and wiped the rest of his tears away. "See, you were crying for nothing." Quentin shook his head.

"Aye, you," I stated sternly. "Don't call your brother a punk. Having feelings and being emotional doesn't make him a punk. It's okay for boys to cry. You're his brother. You don't pick on him for crying and having feelings. That's not what we do. Okay?"

Quentin nodded. "Y'all go ahead and go to bed. It looks like your mother is stressed out for the night."

The boys ran up the stairs, and I sat on the couch for a moment. I looked around the den, and at least it was clean. We have a cleaning service that comes in once a week, and there are still nights where the crib looks like a tornado ripped through it. Having six kids was indeed a lot, but I wouldn't trade it for the world. I went upstairs and tapped on the girls' bedroom door before opening it. Terrionna was asleep, but Omi was on her bed sobbing quietly, and I pushed out a small sigh. When she saw me, she hurriedly pulled the covers up, and I went over and sat down on the edge of her bed.

"What's wrong, Omi?" I asked in a calm tone. She was still in therapy, and she hadn't gotten suspended this school year. I actually thought she was getting better, but something was obviously wrong.

Omi shook her head frantically and looked terrified, which alarmed me. My heart slammed into my rib cage as I forced the covers away from her. Her right hand flew over her left wrist, and I looked at her. "Omi, move your hand."

Omi continued to cry, but she moved her hand as I eyed a fresh cut, and my heart broke. Shorty was only eleven years old, and she was cutting herself. I let out a big sigh and placed my head in my hands. I didn't know what in the fuck I was doing wrong, but I was exhausted. Omi cried softly as I tried to gather my thoughts.

"I'm sorry, Uncle Houston," she hiccuped.

"Why are you cutting yourself, Omi?" I asked her in a gentle tone, and for the first time ever, I was angry with my sister. Why in the hell did she have to do that when her kids were home and would be the one to find her? I had been trying to fix Omi for the past two years, and I wasn't having any luck. She was traumatized. She saw her mother's dead body. She knew that her mother hurt herself because she was sad. How in the hell was I supposed to correct that? I had tried my best, but every time Omi had an episode, I felt like I failed, and I didn't know what to do anymore.

* * *

I talked to my parents, and my mother felt it was best for her to take FMLA for a few weeks and to let Omi come stay with her for a bit. I felt guilty as hell that I almost felt a sense of relief. I felt like I needed a break, but I instantly felt guilty. If Rihanna and Rasheed started acting out one day, would I ship them off to my mom, or would I deal with it? Was I going to further traumatize Omi? Did she feel like I sent her away? All I knew to do was to let my mother try and to increase her therapy sessions.

Omi had been with my mom for two days, and I had been feeling some kind of way ever since. For the second night in a row, I came in, and the twins were asleep, and that also made me feel like shit. Everything was just going wrong. I poured myself a shot of tequila and tossed it back before sitting on the porch and smoking a blunt. After thirty minutes, I was good and mellow, and I climbed the steps to head to the master bathroom, so I could take a shower.

I was so zoned out as I gathered my pajamas and boxer briefs that I didn't realize Cypher was talking to me until she called my name loudly.

"Yo?" I glanced in her direction.

She stared at me for a moment before speaking. "I was trying to ask you if we're still going to Ransom's birthday party in Winter Crest next week? My parents already told me that they'd keep the kids for two days."

"Sure," I mumbled.

"And please don't forget to put that bookshelf together tomorrow."

"Got it."

"It's been sitting in my office for a month now."

"Yeap."

"What's wrong with you?" Cypher stopped putting clothes away and stared at me, waiting for a reply.

"Nothing." I pulled my shirt over my head and removed my jeans, and she was still staring at me.

"I know something is wrong, Houston. Whatever it is just tell me. We can—"

My head snapped in her direction. "You want to know what's fucking wrong? My roof at the shop is leaking, and it's going to take five figures to get that shit repaired. My fucking niece is cutting herself. She used a razor that a person shaves with, and she put a gash in her fucking wrist. I don't know what the hell I'm doing raising somebody else's kids, and I have two of my own that I barely spend time with because I work so much. And I feel guilty, you know why? Because some days, I don't want this shit," I hissed, and I saw Cypher take a deep breath.

We stared at each other for a moment before I went in the bathroom to take a shower. It took everything in me not to punch a hole in the wall. Now, I had gone and snapped at Cypher, and she hadn't done anything wrong. I felt like I was fucking drowning. My pops always made the shit look easy, but was this what having a family was? Being a leader, a protector, and a provider? Because this was shit was a whole damn lot to deal with.

I stayed in the shower for damn near an hour until the water ran cold. When I got out, I only felt slightly better. I just needed another shot of liquor and some rest. I had the next day off, so I could just chill around the house and relax. My mother was coming to pick Terrionna up, so her and Omi could go to the park and spend the day together.

When I went downstairs to retrieve my shot of liquor, I heard Cypher in the kitchen loading the dishwasher. My guilt returned full throttle as I thought back to how I had spazzed on her, and she dealt with a lot herself. She was often alone in the house with six kids, and two of them weren't even hers, but she kept the house running and organized. S She did that shit while taking care of infants that still had a slightly off sleep schedule and that ate every three hours.

I walked into the kitchen and wrapped my arms around her from behind. Cypher stopped loading the dishwasher. "You feel better?"

"A little."

Cypher turned around to face me. "I will get the roof fixed, so you don't have to worry about that."

I drew back. "Yo, Cypher, I can aff—"

"I know what you can do, Houston. I never doubted for a second that you could. But the fact of the matter is, you went out and got us this big ass house that we needed, but you won't let me help you pay the mortgage. You pay all of the bills, you got me a new car, and you take care of six kids. You have proved that you are the king of this castle. You provide for us and do a damn good job of it. But I have money in the bank, and I'm not about to sit back and watch you become overwhelmed. How is that fair?"

I couldn't bitch about being overwhelmed, then deny my woman's help. It was a pride issue, but after I got the roof fixed, my savings would be down to around $10,000, and I wasn't comfortable with that. Not with all the kids and bills we had. Anything could happen, and I'd need way more than ten bands put away in the event of a real emergency. Shit, if something happened and I couldn't work or bring any money in for three or four months, the mortgage alone would damn near deplete ten stacks.

I gave a slight nod. I wasn't all the way comfortable with it, but in that moment, I had to thank God for Cypher.

"As for Omi, I think it would be a good idea if you started therapy too. Do some sessions with her and then do some sessions alone. She's in a fragile stage in her life, and it's just hard for her to shake what she went through with her mother, but she'll be okay. She's loved, and she comes from a supportive family that would do anything for her. Once she learns how to cope with her mother being gone and how to deal with her emotions, Omi will be like a new person. I promise."

I pressed my forehead against hers and wrapped my arms around her. "God knew I needed you."

"You needed me? I'm sure He knew I needed your fine, big dick, deep pockets having ass way more."

That made me laugh. "You going to hell."

"As long as you're with me."

I pecked Cypher's lips, and that turned into a sloppy tongue kiss that had my dick on brick. I hoisted her up onto the counter, and moments later, she was arching her back and gripping my locks as I lapped at her sweet, sticky nectar. Cypher's thighs locked around my head, and I knew she was about to cum.

"Let that shit go," I mumbled into her pussy, and she squealed as she gripped my hair tighter and grinded her pussy into my face.

"Babyyyy," she breathed as I kissed the inside of her thighs.

I straightened up and kept my gaze trained on Cypher as her chest heaved up and down, and she came down from her orgasmic high. My dick was free from confinement in less than a minute, and I was sliding into her while her eyelids fluttered, and her teeth sank into her bottom lip.

"A nigga needed this pussy," I groaned as my thumb traveled back and forth across her clit while I stroked her.

I wrapped one hand around Cypher's neck and squeezed lightly. Her mouth fell open, but no sound came out as I continued to hit her with hard, deep strokes. Her pussy was so moist and tight that I gritted my teeth together as I watched my shiny dick glide in and out of her. Cypher had the prettiest pussy I'd ever seen, and it was damn sure the best that I'd ever tasted.

I leaned in and snaked my tongue into her mouth

and after some nasty, deep kissing, Cypher was moaning into my mouth as she came all over my dick.

"Fucck, Cypher. Shit." I buried my face in the crook of her neck, and a thought hit me. I lifted my head and peered into her eyes. "Marry me." It wasn't the most romantic proposal, but shit, we were living in a huge house together and raising six kids. If anybody should get married, it should be us.

Cypher's brows lifted, but she didn't speak.

"I'm serious. Will you marry me?" I asked as I kept the pace of my strokes.

"Yes, baby. I'll marry you."

I released my seed into Cypher's womb as we kissed and sealed the deal. Your boy was getting married.

* * *

"You aight?" I chuckled the next day as I flipped the chicken on the grill and glanced over at Zeke. My nigga looked like he was about to throw up, and I knew the double shot of Azul that he had in front of him wouldn't be enough.

I woke up that morning to Cypher and the kids gone. Even though we had ended the night on a good note, I knew she was still concerned about me, so she decided to clear the house out for a bit to give me some time alone, and I appreciated that more than she'd ever know. The house was clean when I woke up, so I got dressed, got a workout in, and went grocery shopping for the week. As I was putting everything away, I got the idea to cook on the grill, so Cypher wouldn't have to cook later, and I invited Zeke over. Since the kids weren't home, we were passing a blunt back and forth while I cooked.

Zeke was staring at his phone. A year later, and he still stalked Cresha's Instagram page from time to time. It only took her two months to find out about that baby, and she left Zeke's ass faster than he could blink. The sad part about it was, a week after she left him, ole girl admitted to Zeke that she didn't think it was his baby, and it wasn't. Karma played no games with Zeke, and he was sick as hell. He tried everything under the sun to get Cresha back, and she wasn't going for it. She ended up with a producer, and he had just stumbled across a video of her gender reveal. If my man didn't look so sad, I might have laughed at his ass.

Zeke stared at the phone and shook his head. "Almost six years gone down the drain for an Instagram thot. This broad never had my baby, but she got pregnant by the next nigga fast as hell."

I nudged his shoulder with the back of my hand as I passed him the blunt. "Hit that and get off that girl's page." I didn't feel like I told you so's were necessary, so I was going to leave the shit alone. I knew my nigga was hurt, but he wasn't a bitter nigga, so I felt I could still share my news with him. "I asked Cypher to marry me."

His head shot up. "Say word?"

"Word. My ass got all these damn kids. Why not get married?"

"Aye, I'm with it, my G. That bachelor party gon' be off the muhfuckin' hook. I'm 'bout to start scouting strippers right now. Oh, this shit gon' be epic."

I laughed. "Why niggas always go to the bachelor party?"

"Because that's the best part. Congratulations, homie. This nigga got six kids, and I don't even have one. I'm gon' go find a chick tonight and shoot her club up."

"The older you get, the more terrible your decisions become."

Just as we finished off the blunt, I heard Cypher and the boys in the kitchen. Omi and Terrionna were with my mom. The boys slid the glass door back and came outside. My eyes were damn near slits. The kids knew I smoked. I just didn't smoke in the house with them.

"Hey, Uncle Zeke," the boys gave him dap, making me smile.

The time that I'd been with Cypher, Qori and

Quentin really grew on me. It baffled me how their sucka ass daddy didn't even make an effort to be in their lives. I was at every football game cheering for them like they were mine, and his bitch ass hadn't even been to one game. As usual, they had a football in their hands, and they were going to toss it around the yard. Cypher came outside with one baby strapped to her chest and the other one cradled in her arms. I took Rasheed from her and kissed her on the lips. She was looking too good in an orange maxi dress.

"Oh, you cooking on the grill?" her eyes lit up. "Let me get those baked beans and this mac and cheese going. Hey, Zeke."

"What up? Why haven't you hooked me up with one of your friends yet?"

"Bye, Zeke."

Cypher went back inside, and I laughed louder than I should have. Zeke kissed his teeth and went to play football with the boys while I sat back in the patio chair holding my son watching them.

Chapter Seventeen

CYPHER

"What the fuck?" I whispered as I woke up to the most painful cramps I'd ever felt outside of childbirth. As soon as I came fully to, it didn't take me long to realize that my panties were damp. I looked at the clock on the nightstand and saw that it was almost six in the morning. Sunlight was coming through the blinds, so I tossed the cover back and saw a spot of blood the size of a tennis ball.

I stared at the blood in awe because my period never started that heavy. Since having the twins, I only bled for three days max, and I could wear panty-liners the entire time. I hadn't had a heavy period since before I had them. I grabbed my phone to check my calendar, and it dawned on me that my cycle was almost three weeks late. I nudged Houston, who was sleeping soundly beside me.

"Bae," I called out to him while still staring down at the blood.

"What's up?" he asked in a groggy voice as I continued to stare at the blood.

"I think I'm having a miscarriage," I stated slowly, and his eyes flew all the way open. That woke his ass up.

Houston peered over to see what I was staring at. "Fuck. We gotta get you to the hospital. That's a lot of blood, shawty. I'll feed the twins and get them dressed. We can take the babies to your mom, and the other kids can stay here."

We have cameras inside the house, outside the house, and we have an alarm system. Being that Omi is over ten, and the boys are almost eleven, we let them stay home alone if we aren't going to be gone for more than an hour. I might be at the ER longer than that, but we were going to be keeping an eye on the cameras at all times, and they knew it. Omi lasted a week with her grandmother, and she wanted to come back home with us, so Houston let her, and she'd been doing good. We didn't want to invade her privacy, but we let her know how important it was that we check her body to make sure she wasn't still cutting, and she agreed to let us.

I eased off the bed and headed for the shower, stunned that I was pregnant when my babies weren't even six months old. The crazy thing is, I was on birth control pills. With my hectic ass life, I had missed maybe two in the last month, but I hadn't missed more than that. Houston must have had some potent ass sperm. I didn't want to get an IUD because I already suffered from bad period cramps, and I knew that might make them worse.

I never thought I'd be relieved at the thought of a miscarriage, but there was no way in hell I could have another child right now. I didn't give a damn how much money Houston and I had combined. Our hands were more than full. I wouldn't even consider getting pregnant again unless the twins were like ten, and at that point, who in the hell would want to start over? I prayed that if I was pregnant, I wouldn't be for long. I also knew that Houston and I had to be more careful because what the fuck?

"How do you feel?" he asked after we dropped the babies off. I had put on a super-sized pad because I was still bleeding, and the cramps were hell.

"This shit hurts, and I'm bleeding a lot. It has to be a miscarriage. My period has never come on full throttle like this. If it gets heavy, it's not until the second or third day."

"Aren't you on the pill?"

"Yes. And I only missed two in the last month. I think I need to switch to something else, but I don't want to have bad side effects."

Houston was quiet for a moment. "I'll get a vasectomy."

I looked at him with a slack jaw. "Really? Are you serious?"

"Yeah. There's no need for you to have to fuck your body up with birth control that might not even work when I don't want any more kids. Do you want any more kids?"

"Not really." I was stunned yet relieved by his revelation. I just knew that in another two or three years, Houston would be trying to get me pregnant again.

"Six kids is more than enough. I have two biological kids, a girl and a boy, and that's good enough for me. I didn't participate in creating the other four, but I love them the same way that I love my own."

A smile eased across my face. I couldn't believe he was willing to get a vasectomy, but that would make my life so much easier. For the first time since I woke up that morning, I felt relief. At the ER, it was confirmed that I had in fact been eight weeks pregnant. We were there for about two and a half hours before the doctor released me to go home.

"I have to take some time to heal from this anyway," I let Houston know. "But I suggest you go ahead and schedule that vasectomy because you can't come near me until it's done."

* * *

Two days later, I was curled up on the couch grinning as I looked through all of the photos that I'd taken of Houston and the boys before the father/son ball. All three of them looked fly as fuck, and you couldn't tell me nothing. I posted them on my Instagram, and the likes and the comments went crazy. I lost count of how many people told me the boys should model, and in them wanting to be just like Houston, they were locking their hair, and they wanted wicks.

My phone rang in my hand, and my brows furrowed when Nicks' name came across my screen. That waste of sperm hadn't reached out to me in more than five months. We literally lived life as if he didn't exist because, really, he didn't.

"What?" I snapped into the phone.

"Why does my cousin have to show me pictures on Instagram for me to know that my sons had a father/son ball, and you got some other nigga going with them? You play a lot of fucked up ass games."

I drew back. The best thing for me to do would be to hang up on him and not let him make my blood pressure rise, but I had some things I needed to get off my chest. "I play games? If I played them the way I should, I would have made good on my threat and put you on child support, but it's not worth the hassle. I'm not doing the most to get the pennies that you have to offer. Thanks to a real man stepping up to the plate, my boys are more than good. They love the hell out of that man. You know what they asked me the other day? What should they get him for father's day?"

"Bitch, fuck you and them kids."

I laughed as Nick hung up in my ear. That nigga was mad, and I gave no fucks. He'd been doing my kids dirty for their entire lives, and now he was mad that another man stepped up to the plate and was everything to them that he wasn't. I wished I would pacify and coddle him when he'd never cared about our feelings. I didn't care about him saying fuck me but saying fuck my kids was the last straw. I blocked Nick, and when the boys got home, I would make sure they blocked him too.

The twins woke up to be fed, and Omi and Terrionna wanted to feed them, so I let them help, and then all the kids got baths. Three hours after they left, Houston and the boys were coming back through the door, and Houston had a slight scowl on his face. My heart started pounding because he never got mad at the boys, so if he was angry, they must have showed out. My gaze darted from him to the boys.

"How was the dance?"

"Dad called us mad that we didn't tell him about the ball," Qori answered, and my nostrils flared.

Houston walked up to me and spoke so the boys couldn't hear him. "I don't care if it takes me a year to find that nigga. When I do, I'm beating his muhfuckin' ass." I could almost feel the heat radiating off Houston, and I knew he meant every word he said.

"Nick has issues, and I'm sick of him," I responded to Qori. "He called me too, got mad, and hung up on me. I can't make you guys not talk to him if you want to, but if you don't like talking to him, just block him so he can't call your phone. I hate how the only time he calls y'all is to fuss at y'all about something when he's not even here like he should be."

"Works for me." Qori pulled out his phone to block Nick, and Quentin did the same.

I had been the bigger person all that I was going to be. I was tired of trying to bite my tongue and not be that parent. Fuck Nick.

Chapter Eighteen

HOUSTON

On Father's Day, I woke up to the smell of food. I checked my phone and saw that it was after nine. It was my first Father's Day with the twins, and I wasn't sure what Cypher had planned. I got out of bed and made it up before putting on pajama pants and going into the bathroom to brush my teeth and wash my face. When I walked into the kitchen, I saw a huge spread of food, and I knew that Cypher had breakfast catered.

"Happy Father's Day!" the kids called out in unison, making me smile.

"Thank you."

I eyed the spread of chicken and waffles, scrambled eggs, French toast, bacon, sausage, shrimp and grits, cinnamon buns, fresh fruit, and a strawberry cheesecake. "Damn." I didn't even know where to start.

"Just tell me what you want, and I'll fix your plate. We didn't want to wake you, so as you can see, we already started." Cypher chuckled.

"Give me some of everything. I'm about to sit out back and talk to the trees," I stated, making her giggle. She knew I was going to smoke, and the kids did too. I was gon' get good and high and fuck that food up.

As I sat in my yard and smoked, I took in my huge backyard and reflected on how much my life had changed. I never would have imagined the first time I met Cypher when I did her tattoo that it would lead to this. At one point, I loved Tiesha, but I could have never envisioned all this with her. She was supposed to walk out of my life, and I was glad that she had. I was with exactly who I wanted to be with, and though I got overwhelmed sometimes, I wouldn't trade being a father for anything in this world. I was gon' step about all six of mine.

I went inside and ate the food until I was so full I couldn't move. The kids were excited to give me my gifts, and they got me everything from shoes, to fitted caps, cologne, and a new wallet. Last, the twins presented me with a huge picture that we'd taken the night of the ball. Cypher had gotten it blown up, and it was nice as fuck. I thought that was it, but Quentin stepped forward and bashfully gave me a letter.

"You want me to read it out loud?"

He nodded, and I unfolded the paper.

"Houston, me and my brother liked you from the first day we met you. We thought your hair was cool and you could dress. We also liked how our mom smiled when she came around you. Omi and Terrionna are annoying, but we even like them too." That part made me laugh.

"You do all the things with us that our dad doesn't do, and you buy us all the cool things that we like. We know there are a lot of kids in this house, but we want to be your kids too." My voice cracked, and I had to stop reading for a moment because I wasn't about to cry. I took a deep breath. "We want you to adopt us, and we want to call you dad. If you want us too."

I looked at the boys and chuckled. I had fought it as hard as I could, but I had tears in my eyes. Fuck it. "Of course, I'll adopt you, and you can call me dad. That's the best gift ever."

The boys ran into my arms, and just like that, they were my sons.

EPILOGUE

Ten years later

Houston

"With the first pick in the draft, the North Carolina Panthers select, Quentin Robinson. Quarterback." The crowd went crazy, and all I could do was close my eyes and thank God. I opened them in time to see Quentin with tears streaming down his face and go up to the podium.

"Thank you to the franchise and the coaches for this opportunity. I promise to give all that I have to this team and to play better than I've ever played. I can't wait to make y'all proud and to retire my parents, Cypher and Houston. Thank you."

Quentin walked back over to us and hugged his

mother as she cried. Omi and Terrionna hugged him next, and I knew the twins were home watching him on the TV, as was Qori, who was preparing to fly out because the day before, he'd been chosen to play for the Miami Dolphins.

"We did it," Quentin gave me dap and a hug.

I was the one always telling the boys that it was okay for men to show emotions, but I hated getting choked up in front of them. I didn't blink the tears away, however. "You did it."

"I couldn't have did it without you."

"Bullshit. When I met your mama, you and your brother were already the nicest ones on the field. *You* did this."

"You did more than you know, Houston. You made me the man I am. From the sex talks to staying on me about my grades and hemming me up when I broke curfew. My mom was a great mom, but she needed your help. You came along and changed her life, which made me and my brother happy. I can't wait to retire you. You loved me more than my own dad ever did, and I love you for that."

Quentin was bawling, and that made me cry. I grabbed the back of his head and pressed my forehead into his. Him and his brother were my sons, and nobody could tell me differently. It was us until the world blew.

The end.

I hope you enjoyed this short Father's Day story. I saw the cover, and I just had to do it. Lol.

Made in the USA
Middletown, DE
28 July 2024

58132827R00116